the Rejects of Room 5

D.A. REED

The Rejects of Room 5
by D. A. Reed

Copyright © 2018 by D. A. Reed
All rights reserved.

Cover design by Phillip Lowe. Page layout by M. A. Reed.

ISBN 978-1-387-59150-3

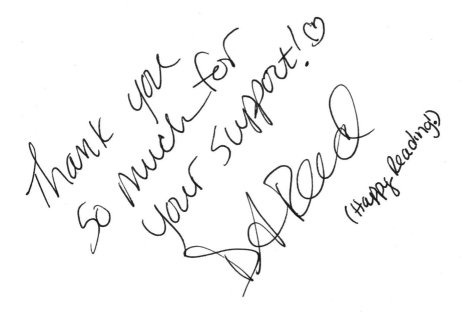

Thank you for so much for your support! ♡

D.A. Reed

(Happy Reading!)

For those who dare to dream and never give up.

D. A. Reed

The Rejects of Room 5

"It sucked – all of it. But I didn't expect anything else."
-Veronica

"Words fail me…"
-Emma
"Hardly. When has that ever happened?"
-V
"Do you always have to have the last word?"
-E
"Yes."
-V

"The growth of a soul can only happen through trials of fire."
-Wallace
"Why do you have to be so freaking poetic all of the time? You're quoting your grandmother again, aren't you?"
-V
"Maybe."
-W

Emma

1.

She was never quite good enough.

That was it. My epitaph. The words that would mark my tombstone and secure my legacy – meager though it was.

Samantha's look was distant. "Sorry, Em. We've already got four."

My eyes darted from Sami to the other three chatting it up, their desks shoved together in a tight circle. None of them stopped talking or bothered to look my way. It figured. Daddy's newfound money had only gotten me so far with the in-crowd.

"Separate into groups of three or four and start brainstorming ideas…"

Sure. Everywhere I looked kids had pushed their desks together and were talking and laughing. If Ms. Hawthorne actually thought brainstorming was happening, she was a little too new at the job.

With dread, I turned to look toward the back of the classroom. My eyes slid closed with equal amounts elation that I wouldn't be working alone, an utter outcast, and dismay at who my partners were going to be.

I had seen the girl with dyed, jet-black hair several times over the years. Her name escaped me. She didn't look too concerned at her lack of partners for the project though, her eyeliner-encased eyes squinting as she picked at the dark blue polish on her nails.

The boy didn't look familiar at all. Walton High was a big school, so I chose that as my defense against complete indifference. My eyes narrowed. He was Mexican or something, his hair dark, skin the color of the tan I always tried for during summer and always failed to achieve. His pants were also two inches too short, and his plaid button down shirt was giving me flashbacks to pictures I had seen of my parents before I was even born.

My head swiveled to stare pleadingly at Ms. Hawthorne, but her head was bent over some papers on her desk. Yet another rebuff to tack on to the rest. Huffing the sigh of the condemned, I shuffled to the back of the room.

Neither the girl nor the boy bothered looking up to see who had invaded their personal space. I cleared my throat. Nothing.

"Hey, it, uh, looks like we're together for the, uh, project."

Eyeliner Girl didn't even glance up from her nails. "What project?"

I stared at her. Seriously?

The boy's eyes darted up in my direction, then back down to the paper he was doodling on before our gazes could make actual contact. "I thought we'd just do our own. You know, individually."

My head shook slowly from side to side, sure I had heard wrong. "Um...we can't. Ms. Hawthorne said we have to work in groups."

The boy shrugged. I finally got a response from the girl. Even though it was an eye roll. I think. It was hard to see past all that eyeliner.

"We'll get marked down," I tried again, feeling panic creep into my voice. I could already hear my father's voice in my head – and it wasn't pretty.

The girl sighed. "Rules are made to be broken," she said drily, reaching up to rake blue fingernails through her hair.

"No, they're not!" I sputtered loudly, my knuckles turning white as I gripped my notebooks even harder. I could feel pages creasing under the pressure.

The boy looked up – I mean, actually *looked* at me – alarm on his face. What, did he think I was going to go crazy or something? I tried to relax the grip on my notebooks. "Okay, we can do it together," he said quickly, his eyes slightly warped behind thick glasses.

His words relieved the tension in my shoulders almost instantly. On the heels of that came a blush that turned my cheeks a nice, flaming shade of red. For being one of the popular kids at Walton, I was definitely acting like a nerd.

Feeling like sitting down might take some of the attention off me, as now even Eyeliner Girl was staring at me suspiciously, I quickly slid into a chair behind the closest desk, banging my knee against the desk leg in the process. My eyes watered from the pain.

"Um, I'm Emma Swann," I said, tossing my blond hair over my shoulder as I carefully pried stiff fingers from around the bent notebooks in my hands.

"Fascinating," Eyeliner Girl muttered under her breath.

I glared. "And you are…?" I purposely left it hanging.

Sighing, she flipped her hair over her shoulder in what I felt sure was supposed to be in imitation of me. "Veronica Bennett," she said, affecting a lofty tone.

It was my turn to roll my eyes. Turning to the boy next to me, I said more gently. "What's your name?"

His bronze skin turned a dull shade of red under my gaze. "Uh, Wallace. Wallace Perez."

Veronica snorted loudly through her nose. "Wallace? Really? Talk about setting your kid up for failure from birth."

I gaped at her. "That wasn't nice," I snapped.

"Oh, like you've never said anything like that before?" Veronica's look could have cut ice. "Sorry, Ms. Swann," she said sarcastically, "but I've walked by your lunch table before."

My face burned. I couldn't deny it; I had done my fair share of making fun of people before. But not to their *face*.

Veronica was apparently done with me; she turned back to Wallace. "We'll call you Ace."

"Uh, okay." Wallace either didn't care about his new nickname, or was too flustered to fight it. Or maybe he was just afraid of Veronica. I suddenly noticed the skin near his left eye was twitching.

Clearing my throat, I shifted my notebooks, choosing the one with the purple plaid cover to flip open. "Okay, so what are your ideas for the project?"

"What project?" Veronica asked absently. She was back to picking at her blue nail polish.

My eyes slid closed as I exhaled loudly. This was going to be a long several weeks.

Wallace glanced at Veronica, then back at me. "Um, I'm open to ideas."

A *very* long several weeks.

Veronica tossed her black hair over her shoulder. "Just pick something cute to research. Otters, or something. Everyone likes otters. For some reason," she mumbled at the end.

Wallace squinted at Veronica like she was a species he had never seen before while I exhaled loudly through my nose. Again.

"We are in sociology class, not zoology class," I said, my lips pulled tightly against my teeth as I fought to keep cool.

Veronica wrinkled her freckled nose and waved dismissively. "Then just find a way to tie it all into the economy of humans, or something like that."

Or something like that? I sat mute, my mind blank of any comeback. I couldn't figure out if the girl across from me was insanely smart and trying to cover it up, or aggravatingly stupid. My gaze shifted to Wallace, perhaps hoping he might save me from the alien species we were deigned to work with, but he simply lifted a shoulder in a baffled shrug.

Thankfully, the bell rang at just that moment, allowing me to avoid having to find words. Veronica shot up from her chair as if it was on fire, snatching her books off the desk and making a beeline for the door without saying another word. Wallace stood more slowly, grabbing a black backpack that lay at his feet.

"Don't worry, we'll come up with something next class," he said, trying to sound reassuring.

It would have helped if he didn't look so worried.

"Yeah," I sighed, closing my purple plaid notebook. "Sure."

I turned, looking for Sami and my other friends, but all I saw were their backs as they walked out the door of Room 5. A shaft of anxiety lanced through me as I fought the urge to chase after them. *Don't make a fool of yourself, Emma.* My father's words, spoken so often they were a constant presence in the back of my mind, forced me to my feet slowly as my friends disappeared into the hallway.

Somehow, being made to look a fool was the least of my worries.

Veronica

2.

Shrugging the strap of my backpack higher onto my shoulder, I shoved through the crowd of students until I made it through the double doors. I breathed in deeply, the cool spring air erasing some of the irritation I felt. Until an inept freshman ran into me from behind.

I swung to the side and planted a hand on the kid's shoulder, giving him a hard shove. "Watch where you're walking, Freshie," I yelled, and felt a small shiver of satisfaction at the shock and fear that crossed his face.

"Hey, Vern!"

My eyes slid closed, the aggravation of the day swallowing me again as the nickname I detested more than anything was yelled across the quad. "What did I tell you about calling me that," I hissed as Liam jogged up to my side. He ignored my irritation and threw his arm around my shoulders. I shrugged, immediately throwing it off and walking away.

"Oh, come on, Veronica," Liam said, his long legs keeping pace with my exasperation-filled stride. "I've got the cigarettes you wanted."

I slowed a bit, slightly mollified. Glancing at him over my shoulder, I reached for the keys of my rusted old Impala. "If you need a ride, get in. I'm not waiting for you."

"You don't gotta be like that." Liam shrugged his pack off and tossed it onto the floor of my car, crunching several discarded candy wrappers in the process. "Clean your car, Vern."

I rammed the key in the ignition. "Only when you stop calling me Vern, Mail."

Liam's eyes narrowed as the Impala chugged and sputtered to life. He hated when I reminded him that his name backward spelled mail. I smirked smugly. Karma and all that.

"So where are they?" I leaned back, eyeing my off again, on again boyfriend. Currently, we were off. Though he liked to ignore that most of the time.

"Geez, Veronica, we're still on school property. You wanna get suspended?"

My stare didn't waver. Liam finally shrugged and dug into an outside pocket of his backpack. "Here you go."

The rectangular box landed on my thigh and I grabbed it, ripping off the plastic wrapping in one move. Liam eyed me. "Rough day?"

The lighter I always kept in the Impala's console flared to life, and I sucked in deeply as the end of the cigarette ignited. "When isn't it?" I blew the smoke out toward the window, then realized it was closed.

Hitting the power lock, I met the eyes of Freshie. I had to give the kid some cred – he was trying to look tough as he walked to his big sister's car. I inhaled again, then exhaled the smoke in his direction. Putting the Impala in gear, I slammed down on the accelerator, grinning as I flipped the kid the bird. The car's tires squealed as I peeled forward, and I barely took the time to look for other cars before roaring onto the road.

"Do I get one? I paid for those, you know."

I tossed the pack toward Liam, not caring where it landed. "Quit whining."

Liam lit his own and then turned to look at me. I ignored him. "What gives, Vern? And I'll keep calling you that until you answer me."

"I'll pull over and leave you on the side of the road," I retorted, the hand clutching the steering wheel turning white.

"You going to drag me out too? Last I checked, I outweigh you by a hundred pounds."

Liam had me, and he knew it. I remained silent for a few more mutinous seconds, then sighed. Taking another hit from my cigarette, I tossed the rest out the window. It wasn't helping the way I thought it would.

"I have to go see the school counselor tomorrow, some jerk stole my last five bucks out of my locker during gym, and now I have to work on some freaking sociology project with Miss Priss and Nerd Boy."

Liam exhaled smoke out his window, his shoulder-length blonde hair ruffling in the breeze. "Rough."

I rolled my eyes. "You have such a way of stating the obvious."

Leaning his arm on the bottom of the open window, Liam winked at me. "I'll gladly make your day better."

"Cool it, Romeo," I snapped. "We're off, remember?"

"When did that turn you into a prude?"

Jerking the wheel to the right, gravel sprayed as the tires of my Impala raked through the unpaved shoulder of the road. I slammed on the brakes so hard both our seatbelts locked. Liam grunted in surprise, and he swiped frantically for his cigarette as it launched from his fingers and into the dirt.

"Get out," I snapped as I sent a glare shooting across the car.

Liam groaned. "Come on, you don't mean that."

Horns honked as other students and traffic had to swing wide to avoid the back end of the Impala where it still stuck out into the road. "Yeah. I do."

"Don't come crawling back to me when you change your mind, *Vern*," Liam growled as he grabbed his pack off the floor and climbed out of the Impala. The door slammed so hard it rocked the car.

"Won't happen," I shouted, then stomped on the accelerator and merged back into traffic amidst more blaring horns.

Five minutes later, I pulled into the gravel drive of our small trailer and got out, slamming the door as hard as Liam had when I dumped him on the side of the road. The rusting metal post and wooden sign with "The Bennetts" scrawled across it were both creaking in the spring wind. Absently, I noted that the pale blue paint on the sign was flaking off.

Skipping the broken bottom stair, I bounded up to the small deck. Sidestepping the sagging board so that it wouldn't break under my weight, I threw open the screen door that no longer had a screen, and put my shoulder into the front door so it wouldn't stick and knock me on my butt on the deck.

I dropped my backpack on the floor just inside the door. "Mom, I'm home!" It was automatic. One of those things your mother tells you to do when you set foot in the house as a kid so she can stop worrying someone snatched you off the playground when she wasn't paying attention.

Yanking the fridge door open, I grabbed a yogurt and peeled back the top. It was when I grabbed a spoon out of the drawer that I saw the note.

**Have to work late. Be home after dinner.
Pizza in freezer if you want it.**
Mom

Sighing, I shoveled yogurt in my mouth and flopped down on the couch. The television sprang to life, and I tossed the remote onto the couch.

The anger was constant now. If someone bothered to ask, I wouldn't be able to tell him why. Well, not *exactly* why. I had a few ideas. But for the most part, it was just there, almost physical. I couldn't erase it, I couldn't dull it; I was its slave.

And I needed a break.

A night without parental supervision. While not new, I was feeling reckless enough to make the most of my situation. The spoon tapped lightly on my lips.

This could be fun…

Wallace

3.

"Play with me, Wally!"

The shout was the only warning I had before my little brother catapulted himself onto my bed – and my homework. Papers went flying, and I almost rammed my pen into my eye.

"Lucas, get out of here!" I roared.

Giggling, my six-year-old nemesis ignored my yell of outrage. Instead, he slithered across my comforter, dislodging my sociology book and all the notes I had been making, and sending them sliding to the floor.

"Lucas, c'mon!" I said, sighing as his little fingers dug into my armpit in an attempt to tickle me. "I'm not in the mood."

Instead of backing off, Lucas stuck his little nose so close to mine that they touched. "Play Bear with me, Wally!" he shrieked.

I winced, my eardrum protesting the noise I could swear broke the sound barrier. "I have work to do, little hermano," I said, trying to reach down to pick up the papers scattered on the floor. But Lucas' fingers found my armpit again, and my arm snapped back in a defensive maneuver.

"I want to play Bear, Wally!"

I felt irritation rush forward so fast, my mouth opened before conscious thought took over. I was barely able to stop the words. Just before I could respond, I really looked at the little guy in front of me. His round face was lit up with excitement, and his wide mouth stretched even farther in a grin.

I sighed. Just because I was mad at the world didn't mean everyone else should be too.

Slanting my eyes, I scrunched my face up into a scowl. "You better run, little boy," I said, deepening my voice to a bear-like growl.

Lucas squealed in delight and launched himself from the bed, his socked feet slipping out from under him as he scampered toward the door as fast as he could. Grinning, I chased after him, letting out roars and growls as I ran through the short hallway and into the living room.

A high-pitched shriek sounded from beside me, and out of the corner of my eye I saw a little body launch off a chair. Gagging as my air was abruptly cut off, I latched onto the small arms now clinging to my neck. Gabby may only be two years old, but she was solid, and her weight hanging from my neck was dangerous to my health. Bending over suddenly, I was able to swing Gabby's little body around until she was in front of me. She shrieked and giggled, her chubby cheeks glowing as she laughed.

"I have you now, little girl," I roared in awesome Bear imitation. "I'm coming for *you*," I growled, pointing toward where Lucas cowered behind the chair holding our grandmother. Or at least, cowering as much as a little boy can when he's grinning ear to ear. "Abuela will not save you!"

"Now wait just a minute, joven," Abuela said, her eyes narrowing in a mock glare. "Don't you start thinking an old woman can't defend herself and her loved ones." I suddenly found myself on the wrong end of a knitting needle as my grandmother brandished it like a sword.

Holding onto Gabby with one hand, I raised the other in surrender and walked backward. "This isn't over yet, boy," I hissed, my face still scrunched into a bear-scowl.

My theatric moment was ruined in the next second as I tripped over Theresa's sneakered feet. "Watch it," my sister snapped in the way only twelve-year-olds can. I should know. I was one not that long ago. Before I could respond, her nose was once again buried in her latest poetry book.

Mateo shuffled the few feet from the kitchen to the living room. "Are you done with your homework yet?" he whined. "I want to look at comic books."

I raised my eyebrows while hefting Gabby higher in my arms. She squirmed fiercely, and I released her. She immediately darted for her rag doll and Abuela's lap. "You can read comic books in our room while I'm doing my homework, you know."

My nine-year-old brother rolled his eyes. "Maybe I like a little privacy every once in a while."

I couldn't argue with that. We were a large family living in a small house. There were times when it felt suffocating to me too.

"I'm done for now; it's all yours," I said as I walked toward the kitchen.

My stomach gurgled as I opened the refrigerator door. Suddenly starving, my eyes skimmed over the meager contents. There were leftover enchiladas from dinner, but I knew Mamá was planning to save those for a meal later that week. As I rummaged through the condiments, looking for something more substantial, whispered voices drifted in through the screened back door.

"Miguel and Sofia had to leave…left baby with…"

My mother's voice was drowned out by a passing car. My hand faltered, landing on a container of tortillas. Who were they talking about? Miguel from down the street? Did they move? My ears strained for more, unease settling over me even though I wasn't sure why.

"Mi nieto."

Abuela's sharp tone snapped me out of my thoughts and also covered Papa's response. I looked at her over the refrigerator door.

"Unless you plan on cooling off the entire casa, grandson, I suggest you choose quickly and close la puerta."

My face heating slightly, I grabbed a container of salsa, closed the refrigerator, and grabbed the tortilla chips out of the basket on the counter. "Sorry, Abuela," I said quietly.

My grandmother gave me a short smile, but it faded as her eyes drifted toward the back door and the darkness beyond before returning to her knitting. Gabby was tucked into the chair beside her, playing with the yarn covering her doll's head for hair.

Carrying my snack to the couch, I stepped over Lucas, who was now playing with some Legos on the floor. Theresa ignored me as I flopped down on the other end of the couch, her eyes intent behind her glasses as they flicked from line to line of her book. Shaking my head, I tore into the chips and salsa.

"Something is on your mind, nieto," Abuela said quietly after a few moments of silence. "Qué? What is it?"

I sighed. "I have to do a project at school for sociology class."

My grandmother kept knitting, the needles clicking together in a rapid staccato beat. I knew that was my cue to go on.

"We have to work in a group."

"Ah," Abuela murmured, a small smile curving her lips.

I glared at her, even though she wasn't looking at me. It unnerved me how well my grandmother knew me. It was like I couldn't keep a secret from her. Ever. Not that I had any secrets.

"I have to work with two girls."

"Mm hm."

I rolled my eyes. "One doesn't even seem interested in working on it, and we haven't come up with a subject yet."

Abuela was silent for so long, I thought she had decided not to continue the conversation. I was about to get up to put away the chips and salsa when she spoke. "You have lived two lives. Uno aquí...one here and one in Méjico. And you cannot find la asignatura...a subject, hm?"

I loved my grandmother, but irritation immediately took over. "I'd rather not do a project that will do nothing but draw attention to me."

Click, click, click. "You do not think the students in your school should come to understand a few things about la patria...your home country?"

"*This* is my home," I said sharply. Theresa's head actually came out of her book, and I saw Lucas' hand pause on the skyscraper he was making. I lowered my voice.

"I don't need any help in revealing how different I am from everyone else, okay?"

"And different...it is bad?"

I breathed harshly through my nose. She just didn't get it.

"It doesn't help, let's just put it that way."

I got up from the couch before Abuela could say anything else, and put away the food. I glanced toward the back door, but I couldn't hear or see my parents. Walking down the hallway, I reentered my room. Mateo may want privacy, but he was out of luck. I had homework to finish, and I didn't feel like getting a lecture while I did it. I closed the bedroom door hard behind me.

Emma

4.

My fingers convulsed around my pencil as Mom's voice rose to a feverish, screaming pitch. Dad's tone was just as sharp, but lower in tone, if not in volume. Dinner had been fun.

Not.

Sighing, I rubbed my fingers over my forehead. I was trying to write in my journal, but couldn't concentrate with all of their yelling. Forcing my hand to relax around my pencil, I stared at the page in front of me. They were fighting so much lately. They always had, but it was worse now, like something had happened that suddenly made them hate each other.

I focused on the words I had just written.

> *The rumble of voices rose and fell in a rhythmic*
> *cadence, swelling and receding like waves on the*
> *shore.*

Yeah, okay. That wasn't too bad. The blunt point of my pencil tapped lightly on the page. What was next?

The words flew from their mouths like birds
roiling in the tumultuous clouds –

Okay, this wasn't working. I threw my pencil down on the desk. Like birds? Really? I couldn't come up with *anything* better?

The door of my room flew open, and my sister came barreling through, throwing herself onto my bed in true dramatic Hailee fashion. I could swear she was thirteen going on thirty.

"I hate this," Hailee said, staring up at my ceiling.

I swiveled my chair away from my desk. Usually I would be annoyed with my sister for barging in without knocking, but at this point – between the arguing and the hideous writing – I was thankful for any distraction.

"I wish we could just leave, you know? Sometimes I feel like running away." Hailee rolled onto her side and stared across the room at me.

I stared back. "So let's go."

Hailee jerked upright. "What? Really?"

Shrugging, I stood up and grabbed a hoodie from the floor. "Why not? They're yelling so loud they won't hear us leave."

"Wait." Hailee suddenly looked uncertain. "You don't mean, leave forever, do you?"

"No, genius," I said, rolling my eyes as I grabbed another sweatshirt and tossed it in her direction. "Let's start with a walk. Then we can contemplate the ramifications of becoming teenage vagabonds."

Hailee wrinkled her nose. "Why do you always use such big words? Half the time I don't even know what you're saying."

I smirked. "Ever stop to think maybe that's why I use them?"

Hailee stuck her tongue out at me before yanking the sweatshirt over her head. Okay, so maybe she wasn't going on thirty. Yet.

We crept down the stairs, although a herd of elephants could have stampeded down them and our parents wouldn't have noticed.

"Like you're ever around!" Mom shrieked.

"Ever think there's a reason why?" Dad yelled back.

My stomach clenching painfully, I grabbed Hailee's arm and dragged her toward the back door. As soon as it slammed shut behind us, we both took a deep breath at the same time. Looking at each other through the darkness, we giggled nervously. Jamming my hands into the front pocket of my hoodie, I set out toward the road.

"So did I tell you about Nate?" Hailee piped up suddenly. "He's a total hottie! His family moved here from…"

I let my sister's words wash over me, content to think about anything but writing or our parents. I loved both, but lately neither one was working well.

Lifting my face toward the sky, I breathed in the cool spring air, wishing life was as easy as sitting back and looking at the stars. A cloud passed in front of the moon, making it even darker for a minute before letting it shine again.

It took me awhile to realize Hailee wasn't talking anymore. I looked at her out of the corner of my eye, feeling bad that I hadn't paid attention to what she was saying. Hailee stared at the pavement in front of her, the expression on her face unreadable. I jabbed her lightly with my elbow.

"Race you."

"What?" She looked up, startled.

"Race you to the park." I was already running, hoping she would follow.

"Hey, no fair!" my sister shrieked, and I grinned as I heard her sneakers pounding on the sidewalk behind me.

Hailee was a fast runner, and I had to really haul to make it to the park before she did. We were both out of breath when we got there and collapsed on the swings. Hailee wasn't done yet though.

"Bet I can go higher than you!" she yelled, already pumping her legs back and forth.

The competitive streak my mom always said I had, and that I always denied having, sprang to life and I kicked off with a vengeance. The wind tugged at my hair as I clung to the metal chains, and I watched the toes of my shoes brush the edge of the moon as I stretched toward the sky. Leaning my head back, I closed my eyes and let the breeze pull away my frustrations.

I felt a lot better when my swing finally slowed to a gentle sway, my feet dragging on the ground. Glancing at Hailee, I could tell she felt the same. I hated to ruin it for her.

"We should head back."

My sister's face fell, then became mutinous. "I don't want to."

"I don't either."

Hailee looked surprised by my honesty. But I didn't want her thinking she was alone in this. Whatever happened with our family, we had to stick together.

"But we have to."

Sighing, Hailee jumped off the swing and shoved her hands into the pockets of her sweatshirt. "You're a horrible older sister."

I assumed she meant for making her go back home. In truth, I felt mean making her go back, but I couldn't say that. Instead, I rolled my eyes. "Yeah, I'm the worst. Come on."

The walk back was silent. It felt like we were walking toward a firing squad, or at the very least, a tornado or some other natural disaster that would eat us up and spit us out again. I didn't want to go home any more than Hailee did, but where else could we go?

It was a lot quieter when we opened the back door. The television blared, which meant Dad was trying to drown his anger in baseball and beer. I couldn't see Mom anywhere, but that was fine with me.

I ushered Hailee upstairs and into her room, pulling my little sis close for a brief hug before shoving her into her room and closing the door. Hearing my parent's bedroom door begin to squeak open, I practically sprinted to my room, not wanting to talk to Mom yet.

Closing the door quietly behind me, I kicked off my sneakers and pulled the sweatshirt over my head. I stared at my journal for a moment, not sure if I wanted to put myself through the torture of failing yet again. Something felt different now, though.

I sat down and picked up the pencil. Then I pushed it into the electric sharpener at the back edge of my desk. Then straightened a few papers. I was stalling. *Just do it,* I scolded myself.

Clouds slid across the glowing orb in a futile effort
to dim the brilliance of the moon. Her soul lifted
as surely as the wind raised the leaves of the tree
with its feather-like touch. Slender fingers dug into
the rich earth, shifting, moving, feeling from
whence she came.

I leaned back, squinting at the words I had just written. Then I smiled, bent forward, and put the pencil back on the paper.

Veronica

5.

I chugged the beer easily. It wasn't my first.

"Dare you," Lindy said again, her eyes shiny from the moonlight, and also from the beer. I loved the girl, but she was a lightweight.

"It's not much of a dare," I scoffed, tilting the brown bottle back again.

"It is when you're drunk." Lindy giggled and popped open her second beer. She was trying to catch up, but she wouldn't. Of all things, she should have realized that by now.

Lindy was great, and I guess you could call her my BFF. If I ever used nerd language like *BFF* – which I don't. What no one knew, even Lindy, was that I could walk away from everyone I knew without a second glance. I wanted it that way.

Just like my father.

Suddenly irritated, I set my second empty beer bottle on the ground harder than I intended and it tipped over, rolling through the short grass of the park to clink against the first bottle. "Watch this," I told Lindy through clenched teeth as I shoved to my feet.

Lindy let out a yell of approval, beer bottle lifted high above her head as I strode through the darkness toward the river. It took me two seconds to realize I had made a really dumb decision.

Two beers down and only having eaten a yogurt cup after I got home from school meant that the alcohol went straight to my head as soon as I stood up. And I thought Lindy was a lightweight. Geez. I tried not to stumble as I walked toward the river. Not to mention it was really dark. The lights along the park path didn't reach this far. My foot caught on a tree root, and I almost went down, curses flooding from my mouth. I could hear Lindy giggling behind me.

"If you're going to laugh, I'll drag you in here with me," I called back over my shoulder, my voice threatening.

"Aren't you in yet? I think you're scared."

Lindy's taunts were like a splinter gouging its way under my skin. Afraid? That was one thing *no one* could call me. I yanked my shirt over my head and stepped out of my shorts. *Three strikes and you're out,* a small voice in my head taunted.

Only if you get caught, I answered back as I stepped into the swirling water. My breath sucked in sharply as the frigid water lapped over my feet.

Being in the park past ten at night, drinking in the park, and now indecent exposure. My mouth tilted in a half smile. The cops could bring it on – *if* they managed to catch me. Most of the PoPo in Walton ate a few too many donuts, if you know what I mean.

"I'm going to push you in," Lindy yelled from the grassy area where she lounged, her second beer already half gone.

"Only if you want to come in with me," I shouted back. Turning back toward the churning water, I took a deep breath.

Alcohol swirled through my system as fast as the water around my ankles, and I felt light-headed, almost like an out of body experience. It made me feel like I could take on the world. Or swim across the turbulent Percel River. Staring across the water, I could barely make out the riverbank on the other side through the dark.

Here goes nothing.

Taking a deep breath, I raised my arms and stretched forward, jumping a little bit to get to the deeper part of the river. It was spring in

Walton, Michigan, and that meant all bodies of water were cold. And by cold, I mean frigid.

As the ice cold water broke over my body, I felt as if the river had sucked all oxygen from my lungs, and I exhaled in shock. Lindy screamed her approval behind me. I slapped at the water, my arms and legs suddenly awkward and numb.

The current was fast, and I felt my body being jerked to the left as I floundered in the water. Something hit my thigh hard enough I was sure it left a bruise, and I swore. My toes stretched toward the bottom of the river, thinking that I could push off and launch myself toward the other side if I could reach, but the current wouldn't let go of my legs long enough to let me straighten them.

A large boulder barely missed my shoulder, water hitting the large rock and rebounding, slapping me in the face. Shocked, I inhaled, and immediately began coughing.

I'm going to die in the Percel River. The thought slid through my mind like a snake through water, and I immediately shut off the fear that wanted to take over. I shut off all emotion; I was pretty good at that.

My teeth ground together, and I used all the strength I had to pull my arms through the water in strong strokes. The current had already carried me quite a ways down from where Lindy lounged on the grass, and I needed to get out. Now.

I managed to gain a couple of inches, but then something I couldn't see in the darkness hit my side, and my body went limp for a second as pain took over. The river took that as an invitation and swept me even farther away. *Come on,* I growled in my head. *Move!*

A couple more inches gained still meant several feet down the river lost. I kicked hard with my legs, using their strength since my arms weren't doing enough. The bank of the river was in sight now, and I kicked and pulled harder. Suddenly, I felt my feet drag through dirt, and I dug my toes in for leverage as I flung my body toward the grass and bushes in front of me.

I had no idea how long I lay there, gasping for breath, shivering in the cool air with nothing on my but my bra and underwear. Then I heard shouting.

"Veronica! *Veronica!*"

Geez, Lindy was going to wake the entire town.

"I'm on the other side," I finally managed to call out, raising my arm from where I was lying so she could – hopefully – find me in the dark.

"Are you okay? What happened?"

I rolled over onto my side, groaning as I felt all the places I was going to have bruises in the morning. If I didn't already.

"The current got me," I said as I stumbled to my feet. At least my ride down the river had done one good thing – I suddenly felt stone cold sober.

"I have your clothes," Lindy said, waving them above her head like a flag. She looked pretty proud of herself, at least from what I could see in the dark. Then she stumbled backward as the beer took over and the frantic motions threw her off balance.

"Great," I said sarcastically. "If only I was over there." Because there was no way I was swimming across that river again.

"Oh." Lindy looked stumped. "Um…"

I peered around, trying to place where I had ended up. There were a few lights on the path to the right that I could see. Was that a bridge?

"Down this way," I called, wrapping my arms around my bare stomach as I trudged through the grass. Geez, I was cold.

I could see Lindy trotting along on the other side. She almost ran into a tree, veering to the left just in time. I shook my head. She was a trip, that was for sure.

My teeth were knocking together by the time we met up at the footbridge over the river. "Thanks," I said, shivering as Lindy handed me my clothes.

"No prob," she said cheerfully.

I glared at her, then flipped my t-shirt around, looking for the neck hole.

"Oh, no," Lindy hissed, and grabbed my arm, yanking me down below the railing of the bridge. My shirt fell in a heap at my feet.

"What the hell, Lind?" I snapped, really irritated now. I was freezing and wanted my clothes.

"It's the freak patrol," she whispered, not even looking at me. Her eyes were glued to something she could see between the railing bars.

My eyes narrowed as I tried to follow her gaze, then widened as they landed on the two police officers walking up the path, flashlights out and sweeping the areas the path lights didn't reach.

Crap. And I was practically naked. Not to mention the beer on my breath.

Lindy must have had the same thoughts, or at least the beer thought. She was practically shaking beside me. "Hate to do this to you, Veronica, but if my dad finds out I've been drinking…"

And with that, she bailed on me. I mean, literally *bailed.*

I blinked, and when my eyes opened, Lindy was already running off the bridge and into the night. Stealth was not her forte – and that was an understatement – as her Converse shoes pounded across the wood of the bridge. She might as well have waved a flag at the cops – "Hey, we're over here! Come get us!"

A shout split the otherwise still park, and one of the cops pointed in Lindy's direction. The other one, though…the other one was staring right at me.

Grabbing my shirt off the bridge, I hugged my clothes to my chest and followed in Lindy's footsteps, although quieter since I didn't have my shoes. Crap, where were my shoes?

I didn't have time to worry about it as I heard answering thumping footsteps behind me. The one guy I wasn't worried about; too many donuts like we talked about earlier. The other cop though…he looked like he went to the gym for fun.

My feet beat a path through the grass, cutting corners as fast as I could, hoping to loose Bicep Man behind me. A rock cut into the bottom of my foot, and I stumbled, dropping my clothes as I instinctively reached out to break my fall.

"Hey! You! Stop right there!"

At least he hadn't used the overrated "Freeze!" comment that you always heard in the movies. He generated a little bit of respect for that. Still, he was crazy if he thought I was actually going to stop.

My clothes were officially donated to the first person who came across them as I pushed off the grass and took off again, my legs and arms pumping like they did when I was on the track team – in another life. As in, for a week my freshman year before I realized half the girls were snobs and the other half were shooting steroids.

"Hey, stop!"

His voice was farther away this time, and I smirked as I pushed even harder, swerving out onto a back road that led straight to the trailer park. Two steps later, I was forced to slow down as the loose gravel bit into my feet with every step. Shooting a glance over my shoulder, I breathed deep as I realized I had finally lost the Ode to Biceps. Still, I jogged the rest of the way home, taking another quick look around before hopping up the deck steps.

Old Mrs. Wilson was peeking out from behind her faded flowered curtain, and I showed her my middle finger before yanking open the screen door without a screen. Her eyes widened and then narrowed in disapproval as she shook her head and dropped the curtain back into place. I didn't feel sorry; the old bat needed to learn to mind her own business.

Shivering, I hurried to my room and pulled on the first sweatshirt and pair of sweatpants I could find. At least Mom wasn't home yet. That would have been interesting, trying to explain why I was drenched and half naked. It wasn't likely she would notice the beer missing. She never did. Or maybe she just didn't say anything. Either way, I didn't really care.

I flopped down on the couch and reached for my phone – and came up empty. Crap. It was in the pocket of the shorts I had dumped back in the park. My fist pounded the couch cushion in frustration. Now I had to figure out how to get it back. If I could even get it back. I definitely didn't have the money to buy a new cell phone.

The doorbell sounded, giving off its usual tone followed by a metallic clank. I sighed, shoving off from the couch. It better not be a salesman, or he would be getting a piece of my mind. Although, on second thought, it was after ten-thirty at night. Who would be out that late selling stuff?

Double crap, I thought, the answer coming a second too late as I swung the door open to reveal Mr. Biceps.

And he was holding my phone.

Wallace

6.

I would talk Mamá into it; there was no question in my mind. I had to make her understand.

Flipping the pamphlet over in my hand, I looked at the cover one more time. *Bernum School of Architecture.* The best college for architectural design and engineering in the world. It said so, right in the pamphlet.

I had to go there; I had to get in somehow.

Pounding footsteps and yells reverberated through the small house, and I stood up from the desk in the room I shared with Mateo. Mamá would be calling for me soon. The front door slammed over and over as my brothers and sisters ran for the bus.

I headed for the hallway, then stopped and turned back to grab my sketchpad off the desk. Pushing my glasses back up my nose, I hefted my backpack higher and walked out of the bedroom.

"Ah, mi hijo – we need to go."

"Yes, Mamá," I said, wishing for the thousandth time that we could afford a second car. I had heard Papá leave early with another construction worker, before the sun even rose. Now I had to drop Mamá off at her first cleaning job several streets away before going to school. I watched Abuela shuffle around the kitchen, her shawl slipping off one shoulder as she got out the flour. Gabby played with blocks on the kitchen floor.

"Mamá …" I hesitated.

When I didn't go on, Mamá glanced up from her purse. "Qué, mi hijo. What is it, son?"

"I have to get my application in now, ahora, if I am to be accepted for this coming year."

Mamá's hands got very still. Frustration made my hand curl around the pamphlet, creasing the heavy paper.

"It's the best school for architecture in the whole world, Mamá!" I was arguing even though she hadn't said a word. "Think of what I could design and have built! The money I could make for our family."

Abuela set a bread pan down hard on the counter, making me flinch. Mamá's face had gone dark, but I didn't know why.

"Get in the car, mi hijo." Mamá's voice was quiet, but it was the way she sounded – like she was scolding me. Only I hadn't done anything wrong.

"But, Mamá -"

"Ahora, Wallace!"

My eyes narrowed as anger swept through me. She wouldn't even *talk* to me about it. I stabbed my glasses back up my nose with a finger and stomped toward the back door. I threw my backpack into the back of the rusted out Ford and flopped down into the driver's seat.

Mamá slid into the passenger side, and I turned the key in the ignition. I wasn't about to give up. "I would apply for financial aid, Mamá. I would get a job to pay the tuition-"

"I will talk with your Papá tonight."

I almost missed it. "What?" I had to backtrack in my mind to make sure I heard right.

Mamá didn't repeat herself, and I was afraid to ask again. I didn't want her to take back what she had said. The rest of the ride was quiet. I was too busy thinking through what I would say to Papá if he said no to the college to say anything more to Mamá.

As I pulled up to the large house she cleaned weekly, Mamá paused with her hand on the door. "As you go through this día, Wallace, you need to remember that life isn't about money."

My hands tightened on the steering wheel. I didn't understand what she meant. Before I could ask, she was out of the car.

"Te amo, mi hijo. I love you."

The door closed, and Mamá walked toward the house, adjusting the strap of her purse as she crossed the driveway. She cleaned several houses on this block and would walk to each house and clean them before making the long walk back home.

I drove the rest of the way to school confused. Why had Mamá said that about money? College took lots of money, especially one as good as *Bernum School of Architecture*. I was willing to work for it, so what was the problem?

The first bell had already rung by the time I walked through the doors of the high school. I felt my glasses sliding down my nose as I walked fast through the halls, dodging other kids as I tried to make it to my locker. I was almost there when my shoulder slammed into someone walking the other way.

"Hey, watch where you're going!"

I looked up to see Bruce Corder glaring at me as he walked backward down the hall. "Lo siento," I muttered, reverting to Spanish as I felt his eyes rake over me.

"You're in the USA, *hombre*," Bruce jeered. "Speak English or go home!"

I failed to see the humor as the friends on either side of him laughed loudly. Ducking my head and hoping they would leave me alone, I opened my locker and began switching books out of my backpack.

As I closed the door and turned to go to class, I saw the girl from sociology class staring at me. What was her name? Vicky? Veronica? I was pretty sure it started with a 'V' anyway. With the morning I had had already, I felt like snapping at her as she kept staring, but something made me stop at the last minute. I pushed my glasses up my nose and took a step toward her.

"Did you need something?" I asked hesitantly. I wasn't sure why I asked. It was something about the way she kept staring at me, almost like she wanted to say something, but didn't know how to start.

Veronica – I was pretty sure that was her name – tossed her hair over her shoulder and narrowed her eyes. "We aren't friends," she said coldly.

I blinked in surprise. "Uh, okay."

"So you don't need to talk to me." She turned on the heel of her black boot and strode away.

So, obviously she hadn't wanted to confide her deepest, darkest secrets to me. I couldn't have read that situation more wrong if I tried. Next time I just wouldn't say anything. Maybe I would just ignore everyone for the rest of the day; it would make my life easier.

The second bell rang. Great. I was now also officially late for class. A part of me wished I was confident enough to say, *Screw it*, and skip school today.

Instead, I walked to class.

* * * *

"Hey, Perez!" Damon looked up from his lunch long enough to jerk his chin up in greeting. "How's things?"

I plopped my brown lunch sack on the table, pretty sure I just heard the apple in there squish the life out of my sandwich. I sighed. The day hadn't imploded like I thought it would – but there was still time.

"Still alive, so that's something."

Damon shoved a hot dog in his mouth, consuming half of it in one bite. "Sorry." He swallowed hard and slurped soda out of the can in front of him. "I got the new Imperial Wars game."

My mood instantly perked up. "Yeah? How is it?"

"Pretty sweet. You should come over tonight and check it out."

"I'm in," I said immediately, and dug into my lunch with more enthusiasm than the flattened peanut butter and jelly sandwich deserved.

"What class do you have next?"

My mood soured just as fast as it had lightened up a couple minutes before. "Sociology."

The other half of the hot dog disappeared into Damon's mouth. "Just let the girls decide; they always have an opinion about everything anyway."

I barely got in a nod before the cafeteria table jerked wildly as Mason's large form settled on the bench.

"Hey, Dudes. What's up?" Mason breathed hard as he fought to pull his bulk around so he could face the table and the two trays laden with food in front of him.

"My house," Damon said, before taking a huge bite of a brownie. "Tonight. Imperial Wars."

"Awesomeness," Mason said, rubbing his hands together. "Now, my darlings, which of you would like to have the honor of being the first to martyr yourself for the great cause?"

I shook my head as Mason grabbed a hamburger and took a huge bite. He talked to his lunch every day, and even though I knew it was stupid, Mason did it so realistically that every day I looked at his food thinking it would answer back.

"Mm, good choice, good choice, dear hamburger." Mason belched and rubbed his hands together once more. "Now, who's next?"

Damon rolled his eyes, but I started laughing. It felt good to let go of the tension. As Mason scarfed down a tuna sandwich, talking to it the entire time, I began to think the day might not turn out so bad.

Emma

7.

Well, this was great. Just awesome.

I glared at my two project partners, though neither of them bothered to notice so they could be appropriately shamed into contrition. *Yeah, how do you like* that *word, Hailee?* I thought to myself as I huffed out an annoyed sigh.

I had been having a pretty good day. Until I woke up. It all went downhill from there, and it didn't look as if I'd see the top of that hill again any time soon.

On a high from my late night journaling – which I thought was some of my best work yet – it took all of ten seconds for me to realize it had been Mom and Dad screaming at each other that woke me up. And that I had overslept, turning my alarm clock off in my sleep. And that I was going to be late for school.

Dad yelled one parting shot, I heard glass breaking as Mom threw who-knew-what, and reality settled over me like the proverbial cloud of doom. I pulled the blanket back over my head. Then sighed and bolted for the shower. It was either that or stay home with Mom, and if the last few months had been any indicator, she would be through a bottle of wine before lunch.

"Where's Hailee?" I asked, shouldering my backpack as I jogged into the kitchen.

Mom grabbed the corkscrew from a drawer and slammed it back closed. She shrugged. "I think she caught the bus."

My eyes narrowed. "Do you know for sure that she got on the bus?"

The corkscrew slammed down on the granite countertop. "I'm sorry, who's the parent in this room?" Mom's face turned red faster than I knew was possible.

Knowing my answer wouldn't calm her down, I locked my jaw shut and grabbed a banana from the bowl on the far side of the island counter. Snatching my car keys from the hook next to the door, I walked out the door without another word.

Throwing my backpack into the passenger seat, I slid in behind the wheel, pulling my cell phone from my back pocket as I did.

U make it to school ok? I texted, praying my sister actually was at school and that some random weirdo off the street hadn't kidnapped her while Mom and Dad were too busy screaming at each other to notice.

Yeah. It's cool.

No, it's anything *but* cool, I thought, but kept that to myself and breathed a sigh of relief that Hailee was okay.

Turning the key in the ignition, I rammed the car into reverse and tore down the driveway, narrowly missing the garbage can Dad must have wheeled to the bottom sometime that morning. I broke every speed limit there was on the way to school, and for the first time didn't feel guilty about it.

I still didn't get to school until halfway through first hour, and I sprinted into the building, knowing I would be officially marked absent for the first class. My dad was going to freak out. Literally freak out. I wasn't sure why I hurried so fast to get to a class I would be marked absent for, even if I showed up. Except that old habits die hard; if you were supposed to be someplace, you better show up and shut up. I could hear my dad's voice like he was standing right next to me.

"Ungh!"

All the air left my lungs in a harsh exhale as I plowed into someone coming out of the counselor's office.

"Watch it, Priss!"

The apology that sprang to my lips died a violent death as I stared in disbelief at Eyeliner Girl from sociology class. What was her name again? Vanna? And what did she just call me?

"Excuse me?" I asked, slowly straightening to my full height.

Eyeliner Girl's lip curled in a sneer. "I didn't stutter." She turned on her black-booted heel and walked up the hallway.

What a –

I stopped myself just in time. Don't sink to her level, my mind scolded me. Even with the mental admonishment, three snappy comebacks surged forward in my mind. All too late, of course.

The day only got worse from there.

"Anyone? Anyone at all?" I asked through clenched teeth. I was trying hard to control my temper, but I literally felt like I was wound so tight I would fly apart any second. "We need an idea for this project, guys."

"Loosen up," Veronica sneered. I had remembered her name two seconds before Ms. Hawthorne took attendance. "It's not like it really matters, anyway."

Wallace kept his nose buried in his sociology book. He had been flipping pages back and forth for forever now. I wouldn't have minded, if it meant he was looking for project ideas. However, he hadn't said a word the entire class period, and we were about to end class yet again without a project.

If looks could kill, Veronica would have keeled over at her desk. Her attitude was bad enough, but tack on what she called me earlier that morning...I felt like daggers were literally shooting from my eyes. Unfortunately, they weren't, and Veronica continued to chew her gum with the loudest smacking sound I had ever heard.

"It matters," I ground out through my teeth. "Every grade matters." Then I felt something inside me snap; call it too much tension for one day. "What is wrong with you, anyway? Don't you care about anything?"

Veronica abruptly stopped smacking her gum as she pinned me with a glare that made my face heat as if it was on fire. "You don't know *anything* about me, Priss. So I'd keep my mouth shut if I were you."

Wallace finally glanced up from his book, but it looked like he wished he was anywhere but in sociology class.

Veronica had been so anti-social, I didn't really expect her to respond. The venom in her voice left me speechless, and I gaped at her with my mouth partially open. She didn't seem to need an answer though; grabbing her backpack off the floor, she glared at me one last time, her lip curling, then walked out of the classroom. I watched Ms. Hawthorne chase Veronica into the hall. I could only imagine how well that would go.

A cramp in my hand suddenly made me realize how tightly I held my pencil. As I looked down, my hand shook, and I willed it to stop before Wallace could see. Or, worse, Sami and my other friends.

Taking a deep breath, I glanced at Wallace out of the corner of my eye. He was staring at the sociology book again, but the pages were still. The muscles in his jaw were moving like he was clenching and unclenching his teeth. Was he mad? Was he angry that my outburst caused Veronica to leave, ending our chance to figure out our project?

The rest of the groups were talking, their noise a constant hum in the room. Someone threw a wadded piece of paper at the trash and missed. The digital numbers on the clock flipped. Three minutes before class ended. Tension tightened the muscles in my shoulders until I felt physical pain. I was so engrossed in my own thoughts, I actually jumped when Wallace sighed next to me.

"Use my family."

"What?" I automatically leaned closer so I could hear better, even though he was only two feet away from me.

Wallace sighed again and slapped his book closed. "My family is from Mexico. We moved to the United States when I was five. If I have to explain the cultural differences and why this would make a good project, I don't think I want you as my partner."

My mind clicked along so fast it almost derailed. I certainly didn't pay much attention to his rather rude last comment. I was too happy to have something I could work on.

"This is great," I said, flipping open a notebook, ready to ask him some questions right then and there. Then the bell rang.

Wallace shoved his book in his bulging backpack and slid out of his seat. "Yeah, great," he said, his voice flat.

I practically bubbled with excitement. "We'll plan it out tomorrow, okay? Then each of us can work on part of it over the weekend. Sound good? Oh! When can we meet your family? We'll need to interview them." I had to run to keep up with Wallace as he left the classroom and took off down the hall.

Shrugging, Wallace kept his eyes straight in front of him. "Don't know. Not today." He sped up and swerved in between two groups of kids, effectively cutting me off and leaving me in the dust.

I stared at his dirty backpack as it bobbed down the hall away from me. It had a hole near the bottom. As I watched, a pencil slid out and disappeared into the swirling mob of students. What was up with him, anyway? And Veronica? It seemed like everyone needed to chill out today. Me? I was good. Great, in fact. I hated having to rely on other people for things, but at least we had something we could work toward.

I felt much better as I hurried down the hall to Advanced Physics. My mind whirled with ideas, alternately filing and discarding questions to ask Wallace's family. Then I turned a corner and ran right smack into Veronica.

Again.

Veronica

8.

I was pissed. To the point of actually seeing red flashes in front of my eyes.

Poor Emma. Poor, poor rich Emma Swann. She thought she had run into me by accident. I could see her mouth opening to apologize. That's when I shoved her. Hard.

"Hey!" Emma's shout was lost in the jokes and shouts of the other students as she stumbled backward. Such a pity; she managed to regain her footing.

"You got a problem with me, Miss Priss?" I yelled. I didn't care who heard me. But for as much as high school students are up in everyone's business, they're also so engrossed in themselves they don't notice what's going on right under their noses. No one even glanced in our direction.

"What is wrong with you?" Emma yelled right back, shifting her pack back onto her shoulders.

"You. You're what's wrong." I waved my hands in front of me to encompass her entire being. "You think you know me? You don't know anything about me!"

"Really?"

I could see it rise up in her eyes. Fight. She was going to fight. And I wanted one.

"*That's* what you're so pissed about?" Emma sneered. "Grow up, Ms. Eyeliner. Or better yet – why don't you start caring about something besides your nail polish?"

Oh, she did *not* just go there. I took a step toward her, but Emma wasn't backing down.

"Hey! Break it up!"

Both my head and Emma's swiveled to see Mr. Sietsma, the algebra teacher, walking toward us. We glanced back at each other. Emma looked confident that she wasn't going to be the one ending up in the principal's office. As much as it grated on my nerves, I knew she was right. Still, I wasn't going to let her think this was over.

Jerking my chin upward, I hissed, "When you think I don't care about anything," I said as I started to walk backward, "remember that I care enough to hate you and everything you stand for." I looked her up and down derisively, then smirked and turned on my heel, making my way far, far away from Ms. Emma Swann.

Shrugging my pack higher, I forced my way through the crowd, not caring who I trampled to get to the side door I had my gaze locked on. I pushed the doors, throwing them wide, the March sunshine barely diminishing the Michigan cold of early spring.

I didn't feel the cold. I didn't feel anything but rage. My blood was boiling, and it felt like ants were crawling along my skin. The problem remained that I was literally itching for a fight; and the person I wanted to fight was back inside the school.

"Hey, Veronica! Wait up!"

I didn't wait. I was pissed at Lindy too, and I wasn't about to go easy on her.

"Veronica! Geez, I'm sorry okay? You know how my old man is! He'd take my phone, my car – *everything* if he found out I'd had a couple beers! You're so lucky that your mom doesn't care. Or if she does, that she's not around to punish you." Lindy huffed out a laugh, her breath coming hard as she finally caught up to me.

My stride hitched slightly, then I tightened my jaw and kept walking. Lucky, huh? Yeah. I was *so* lucky.

"Can you slow down a bit?" Lindy gasped.

That finally made me stop. "Slow down? *Slow down?* Did you slow down last night? I seem to remember you disappearing without a backward glance while I was surrounded by cops and half naked."

Lindy's eyes widened. "They caught you? V, I thought you were right behind me, I swear!"

I rolled my eyes. Right. "I made it to the trailer, but then Bicep Man showed up at the door with my phone."

A short burst of laughter flew between Lindy's lips before she could stop it; a nervous tic since she was a kid. "Um, obviously he didn't arrest you...?"

I imitated her tic, my lip curling derisively. "Well, since I was fully clothed by the time he showed up, he couldn't really recognize me for sure, you know, with it being dark in the park and my albino white skin blinding him as he chased me and all."

Lindy tried hard to stifle the laughter this time; she kept her mouth closed and it came out through her nose in a snort instead. "Um..."

Tossing my hair over my shoulder, I glared at my best friend. "So I gave him some line about my hair being wet because I just got out of the shower, and *'Oh, thank goodness you found my phone! I lost it the day before when I took a walk in the park after dinner!'*" I fluttered my eyelashes innocently and raised my voice an octave to put on the show I had for the police officer the night before.

Lindy's mouth dropped open. "He bought that?"

I shot her a dirty look. "He didn't have any evidence otherwise unless I decided to strip so he could identify my underwear, so what could he do?" I started walking again.

Hurrying to keep up, Lindy was silent for several seconds. I knew what she wanted to ask next, and I hoped she was wise enough to keep her mouth shut.

No such luck.

"How did the meet with the counselor go? What'd she want, anyway?"

My teeth ground together, but I forced them apart and tried to act nonchalant. "Nothing big. Just needed to make sure I had all my credits before the end of the school year."

Lindy's eyes narrowed as if she didn't believe me. I tried the oldest trick in the book – deflection. "Aren't you supposed to be in class?" I asked, glancing at her out of the corner of my eye.

"Aren't you?" she shot right back.

I sighed. "Come on," I muttered, and led Lindy toward the football field. We hopped the short entrance gate and wound our way to the grassy area behind the bleachers. Little kids always played back there during football games in the fall.

"Awesome," Lindy breathed as I pulled a bag of hand-rolled joints out of my pack. "I need something to take the edge off today."

I swallowed my snarky response and passed her the bag after taking a joint for myself. Flicking my lighter, I breathed in deeply as the marijuana ignited. It needed to work quickly; I needed to mellow out, and fast. Lindy leaned back on her elbows and stared at the clouds, her brown hair dragging on the ground behind her.

Drawing in another hit, I tossed my arms over my knees and stared toward the woods. As much as I hated Miss Priss back at the school, I was doing exactly what she accused me of. Not caring. Yet, I could still hear Ms. Anderson's voice in my head.

"I'm sorry, Veronica, but even if you receive full points for every assignment and test from now until the end of the school year...I can't be sure that you will graduate."

Another drag, and I finally felt the pot start working. At least, I didn't feel like going psycho on Ms. Anderson and the entire counselor's office anymore. Right now anyway.

I could sense Lindy watching me. She knew there was something else going on. For someone who would bail on her best friend and was a lightweight with beer, she was actually pretty smart. There wasn't a lot that got by her.

Why didn't I tell her about the conversation with Ms. Anderson? Because I knew what she would ask next.

Why do you care?

As I sat there and got stoned smoking pot and stared at the woods, all I could think was...

I don't know why I care...but I do.

Wallace
9.

"Mrs. Wright, you are savage!" Mason's eyes lit up with desire and excitement as Damon's mom shifted plates around and put a platter of chicken wings in between the mozzarella sticks and brownies.

Even though she looked slightly confused, Mrs. Wright smiled and winked before heading back up the stairs. Mason had already grabbed a plate and was loading it to capacity. I snatched a plate before he could fill them all and snuck a hand in here and there, trying to get some food before it all disappeared into Mason's endless pit he called a stomach.

"Game's set!" Damon called from across the room. "Hey, Wallace, grab me a brownie!"

"Sure." I reached for the last brownie on the tray at the same time as Mason. As our hands collided, Mason looked at me guiltily, then removed his and took the towering plate in his hand over to the "gaming station," as Damon liked to call it. I grabbed the brownie and headed over to join them.

"Here," I said, handing Damon the brownie. Half of it was promptly demolished as he tossed controllers to me and Mason with his free hand.

"So we all know the rules, right?" Damon asked around his mouthful of brownie.

Mason and I nodded. The three of us had been researching this game for months – since we heard it was coming out. We were ready.

"Game on!" Damon yelled, and the television screen roared to life.

Excitement rushed through me as my fingers navigated the buttons. I loved video games. The adrenaline rush was awesome, and everything seemed to fade away while I played. Nothing existed except the game.

We had been playing for a long time when I saw it. Our characters in the game were approaching the high tower, about to kill the evil king and set the kingdom free, when I saw Mason's hand move from the corner of my eye.

"Nuh-uh." I shook my head, my eyes still locked on the game.

"Duuuude," Damon hissed, knowing without even looking what Mason was doing.

I could see Mason's hand falter as he moved it from the controller, but then it moved again.

"Don't do it, man," I warned, my eyes narrowing as my guy on the screen jumped down a flight of stairs to engage a castle knight.

"But...I can reach it – I know I can-"

"Dude!" Damon yelled, jumping to his feet as Mason's character was run through with a sword. "What are you doing?"

My jaw tightened as more castle knights flooded through the doorways. It was like Mason's death triggered something in the game. Damon and I were screwed; we had barely been holding them off with *three* players.

"Sorry," Mason mumbled, only looking slightly guilty. He had shoved an entire mozzarella stick into his mouth at once. "They were getting cold," he muttered defensively.

It took thirty seconds for us to be cut down by the castle knights and *Game Over* to flash on the screen. Groaning, we threw our controllers onto the floor and glared at Mason. Mason, however, reached defiantly for a chicken wing.

"They. Were. Getting. Cold," he repeated with precise enunciation. "We can't have that, now can we?" he asked the chicken wing in his hand.

Damon threw his hands up in the air, then rammed a finger in his friend's direction. "You make me lose again because of a piece of fried cheese and I swear I will tell my mom never to make you food again. Ever."

I had to swallow a grin as Mason's face twisted in a look of horror. I felt kind of bad for the guy. Kind of. He did make us lose…because of a mozzarella stick. "Hey, Damon, cut him a little slack. We can always play again tomorrow. Without snacks," I said, leaning over to shoot a pointed look in Mason's direction.

Our friend looked wounded that we would take away his most prized form of entertainment and life source, but Damon looked slightly mollified. "Yeah, all right. I guess." He glared at Mason. "No food."

"I don't know what their problem is – don't listen to them, my sweets," Mason crooned to the brownies on his plate as he heaved his bulk off the couch. "They don't know what they're saying…"

Damon shook his head as Mason made his way back over to the food table. "He does know that he still has food on his plate, right?" he asked. "I mean, he's *talking* to it."

I grinned. Mason seemed a little crazy to a lot of people, but I loved the guy. Neither he nor Damon ever looked at me funny because of my skin color, or the fact that my clothes didn't fit right, or that my family didn't have a lot of money. In fact, Mason sat on the one kid who dared call me a Spic back in middle school. Actually *sat* on him. I'm still surprised the kid didn't die. Or at least suffer from a fractured back.

"So we're on for tomorrow night, right? We'll get it this time, I know it." Damon was already back into war-mode.

"Yeah, sure." I shrugged. "But, seriously, don't let your mom make any food."

"Why can't I make any food?"

The three of us jumped as Mrs. Wright came down the stairs holding a tray of homemade pizza rolls. She looked uncertainly at the food she was carrying.

"Did something taste bad? Didn't you like it?" Her eyes passed over the table littered with empty dishes and crumbs, then landed on Mason, whose eyes were locked on the pizza rolls like a man starving.

"Let me help you with those," Mason said, lumbering forward to take the tray.

Damon rolled his eyes. "It was fine, Mom. Mason just has a one-track mind when food is around." He glared at Mason as he shoved a pizza roll in his mouth. "Which made us lose the game."

Mrs. Wright exhaled loudly through her nose, then reached over to pat Mason on the shoulder. "Don't pay any attention to Damon. Eat as much as you like."

Mason took that as an invitation and quickly shoved another pizza roll into his wide mouth, then squinted at Damon as if to gloat that Mrs. Wright was taking his side.

"Oh, Wallace, I have a box of clothes for you to look through. I'll go get it so you can see if there is anything your family might like."

Surprised, I wasn't sure what to say as Mrs. Wright turned to go back up the stairs. "Um, okay." Too late, I realized it would have been polite to offer help carry it downstairs. I looked at Damon, who shrugged.

"Don't look at me. She was on a cleaning kick or something. She took half my clothes and most of Dani's and Leena's too."

I didn't have time to answer before hearing Mrs. Wright's feet on the stairs. As she came into view, I sprang into action, the box so big she couldn't even see the stairs or her own feet. Grabbing the huge box, I maneuvered the rest of the stairs and set it on the floor.

"Whew, thank you, Wallace." Mrs. Wright said, wiping her forehead with the back of her hand and leaving a dirt streak in its path. "I forgot how heavy that was."

I shifted from one foot to the other and ran a hand through my hair. I felt really uncomfortable; no one had ever done something like this before, and I wasn't sure what I was supposed to do.

"Go ahead and look through it," Mrs. Wright urged. "There should be something in there that would fit each of your sisters and brothers, as well as yourself. I included a few of my things and of my husband's in case they would work for your mom and dad." She popped the flaps of the box open.

Bending at the waist, I began sifting through the contents. She was right – there were a lot of clothes, and in all different sizes. It was overwhelming. My mind spun as I tried to remember what sizes my brothers and sisters wore.

Mrs. Wright must have sensed my confusion, because she suddenly put her hand on my shoulder and flipped the box flaps closed again. "You know what? Why don't you just take the box back home and go through it with your family. Anything you don't want you can donate."

"Oh. Okay. Thank you." My feet were shuffling again. "This is really nice of you. You didn't have to-"

"Nonsense. You're doing me a favor by helping me de-clutter my house!" Mrs. Wright laughed and waved her hand in the air. "I'll have Mr. Wright put this in your car."

"Oh, I can do it," I said hastily, reaching for the box.

"No, he has to leave for a meeting in just a few minutes anyway. He can do it so you can have more time with the boys." She flashed me a smile and headed back toward the stairs.

"Hey, bro, got time to do one more round?" Damon waved a controller in the air.

I glanced at my phone and shrugged. "Sure, why not?"

"Sweet!" Mason headed back toward the couch, his plate once again filled to capacity.

Damon and I yelled in unison. "Put the food down!"

Emma

10.

I swirled my straw around in my vanilla milkshake. Sami, Tiffany, Ian, and Ben were sitting in the booth with me, but I found there was a difference between being *with* a group of people and being *included* in a group of people. Turns out there is a big difference in those two words.

"So, I'll pick up the girls and we'll head over about eight, okay?" Sami tossed her hair over her shoulder, then leaned forward to clamp her pink lipsticked lips over the straw poking out of her cup.

Seeing the sharp contrast of the lipstick against Sami's skin made me think of Veronica and the dark lipstick she wore. My mood soured even more, and I shoved my milkshake away from me.

"You're coming, right, Em?"

It took me a second to realize Ian was talking to me. Surprised, I stared at him for a minute before answering. "Um, going where?" I had been so caught up in my own thoughts, I hadn't been paying attention to their conversation. Not that they made an effort to include me.

Tiffany rolled her eyes. "To the *party*, Emma," she said, condescension dripping from the words.

"You know, at Ben's house," Sami prompted me, her voice slightly kinder than Tiffany's. I think she just felt guilty for excluding me from the sociology group project.

"Oh, right." My eyes flashed over to Ben, who was much too interested in the cute redhead who had just walked through the door to notice my gaze. "Um, I guess."

"I only live a few streets down," Ian said, his eyes still on me. "Why don't I come pick you up? That way Sami doesn't have to drive all the way from Brookside."

Sami looked at him sharply, then at me, her eyes narrowing. So much for the kindness born out of guilt. I avoided her gaze, still ticked about the project. What grated even more was Ian's comment about driving all the way from Brookside. I always thought Dad was joking when he talked about "old money" and "new money."

It wasn't long after I was accepted into the in-crowd that I realized the two miles separating Brookside – the neighborhood containing residences for those families whose money came from grandparents with four "greats" in front of the word – might as well have been a hundred miles from Townlin, where I lived. Where families like mine had fathers who suddenly invested at just the right time, or sold a software design at just the right moment.

Established versus new; old money versus new money.

Both sides may have dollars in their bank accounts, but the worlds we resided in might as well have been on different planets. I was part of the in-crowd now, but at the same time, I would never be fully accepted.

So please, let's spare Sami the trauma of having to drive herself from established Brookside to the lowly Townlin neighborhood. Quite suddenly, I had had enough.

"I'll think about it and let you know," I said abruptly as I shoved back from the table.

Tiffany's scandalized gasp was nearly drowned out by Sami's overly loud, "What?!" Ben was finally paying attention. Had anyone opted out of going to one of his parties before? Doubtful.

I couldn't read Ian's look as I grabbed my string bag and turned away from the table. For tonight at least, I was tired of trying to do everything right.

* * * *

It seemed like all the lights were blazing as I pulled up to the house fifteen minutes later. I don't know why that seemed odd to me, but I hesitated for a second before turning off the car. Finally, I grabbed my bag and headed toward the mudroom door.

As soon as I opened the door, I heard the yelling.

"Get out! And don't bother taking your keys – I'm changing the locks!" Mom screamed.

"Change the locks and you'll be hearing from my lawyer," Dad yelled back.

Suddenly there was a huge crash, then the sound of Mom crying.

Dropping my bag on the floor, I bolted into the kitchen, made a hard left, and ran into the living room. Skidding to a halt, I stared in disbelief, my chest heaving from my race through the house.

Dad was just straightening up from a crouched position, wine dripping down the door behind him. Glass shards were sprinkled in his hair and littered the ground near his shoes. Mom was sobbing, tears running down her cheeks even as she stood and stared defiantly at my dad.

"What the hell, Marcia?" Dad roared as he carefully brushed glass out of his graying hair.

"Like you have the right to ask me that," Mom ground out through clenched teeth.

"Mom? Dad?" I couldn't think of anything else to say. Stunned, I finally focused on the suitcases piled at my dad's feet. "What's going on?"

Mom glanced at me, swiped at her cheeks with the backs of her hands, and glared at Dad. "Yeah, Brian. Why don't you tell your daughters what's going on?"

Daughters? I scanned the foyer, my gaze finally landing on the steps leading upstairs. My heart sank as I saw Hailee crouched on the polished landing, her fingers as white as her face as she peered through the bars.

Dad's eyes became slightly less venomous as he looked at me, then quickly away. "Marcia, I don't think-"

"What?" Mom cocked her head mockingly. "You don't think what? That your daughters need to know what a bastard their father is?"

My eyes flew from my mother's hateful gaze to where my father stood tight-lipped by the door. "Dad?" My voice came out small and uncertain.

"Come on, Brian. If you think you had such a good reason for sleeping around, the girls will understand. Right, Emma? Hailee?" Mom turned and swept her arm in our direction, but I don't think she actually saw us.

I looked at Dad, who finally seemed embarrassed. It felt like someone had just punched me in the stomach. I wanted to run, but my feet felt cemented to the floor. Dad was cheating on Mom? It was like I was watching a scene from a movie, of someone else's life. The scene where I always breathed a sigh of relief that it wasn't happening to me. Only now it *was* happening to me.

What was worse was that Mom couldn't seem to shut up.

"Tell them, *honey*," she sneered sarcastically. "Tell them how once you made a whole bunch of money and got a secretary, you decided to follow in your Daddy's footsteps and screw around."

I stared at Mom, then at Dad. Papa cheated on Nana? But they were still married...I felt like my world was imploding, and I didn't know what to do. A muffled sob was my answer.

Finally getting my feet to unstick from the floor, I turned and ran up the steps. Mom was still yelling, but I didn't care. I didn't want to hear it – and I knew Hailee *shouldn't* hear it. Grabbing my sister's arm, I hauled her away from the landing and into my bedroom.

Hailee pulled her arm free as soon as we closed the door, then collapsed on my bed as tears rolled down her cheeks. "Are they going to get divorced?" Hailee scrubbed at her tears with the arm of her sweatshirt, but they kept coming. A hiccup followed.

I stared at my sister, the silence in the room broken by the yells and screams from downstairs – and finally, the slam of the front door.

What was I supposed to tell her? If I lied and they did get divorced, Hailee would hate me forever. If I told her the truth – that I thought they would – she would be inconsolable.

We both shifted our eyes to the door separating us from the rest of the world, and I felt a sudden and furious anger toward my parents for putting me in this position.

* * * *

I closed the door softly behind me, hoping Hailee wouldn't wake up. I didn't care if she spent the whole night in my room; I just didn't want to see the pain in her eyes anymore.

Tiptoeing down the stairs, I prayed Mom had gone to bed. I had drifted off next to Hailee for a while, so I wasn't sure where Mom was. All I knew was that I was starving and needed something to eat.

The house was dark, giving me hope. Moving noiselessly into the kitchen, I felt like I was having a heart attack when I reached for the door handle and heard, "How's Hailee?"

Squinting, I saw Mom sitting at the small breakfast nook in the corner, the shadow of an empty wine bottle next to her on the table. "Mom? I thought you were in bed." I reached over and flicked on the light.

Mom threw her hand up to shield her eyes from the brightness. It was as if she hadn't heard me. "How's Hailee?" she slurred again, regret thickening the words even more. "How's my baby doing?"

Sighing, I bypassed the refrigerator and went straight for the ice cream in the freezer. "She's fine," I lied, taking a spoon from the drawer in front of me. *About as fine as I am,* I mocked silently in my head. *Thanks for asking.*

Mom's arm came down on the table, almost knocking the wine glass and bottle over. "You shouldn't have had to hear all that," she said thickly, remorse causing her eyes to fill with tears.

I paused with a spoonful of ice cream halfway to my mouth. For a second I thought she might actually be apologizing, but then she reached for the wine glass and I knew what was making the words fall from her lips. Mom as a drunk was a sad sight. Even though I didn't want to, I slid into the seat across from my mother and loaded up my spoon with more ice cream than I could fit in my mouth; but I was sure gonna try.

"He's changed. Your father," Mom added as an afterthought. She took another gulp of wine. "I don't...I never expected..."

I watched as Mom's expression slackened and her head drooped toward the table. In the next second she passed out. Pity nudged my emotions, but I shoved it away. There was still too much anger to let pity in too.

As I contemplated the top of Mom's messy hair, a memory of what we were like as a family before Dad made a whole bunch of money came into my head. We would play Monopoly for hours at the dining room table, eating popcorn and drinking lemonade. When was the last time we played Monopoly? Or any game at all? Not since we moved into this place. I couldn't even remember the last time we ate dinner together.

Mom thought Dad had changed? I stared at the wine bottle and thought back to Veronica's snarky comment about walking by my lunch table and hearing comments I made about other kids.

Maybe he wasn't the only one who had changed.

Veronica

11.

"Veronica Bennett, what are you doing?"

I froze for a split second at getting caught, then realized I didn't care. Joint hanging from one hand, beer from the other, I tossed a bored glance over my shoulder toward my mom's silhouette in the doorway. "You're home early." It was a matter-of-fact statement, no real emotion because I didn't feel any. I thanked the combo of pot and alcohol for that.

"Put that out *now*. Then come inside. We obviously need to talk."

Her shadow disappeared, and light from the kitchen once again spilled out onto the back steps of the trailer where I sat. My eyes closed briefly as I ran through the options in my head, but it turned out there weren't that many. I rammed the joint down onto the step, effectively cutting off its glow, then defensively clutched my beer a little harder and got up to go inside. She hadn't said anything about getting rid of the beer.

Mom was already pacing by the time I flopped down in the old brown recliner. I felt it give slightly, and was surprised when it didn't collapse and send me sprawling onto the floor. Small miracles.

"Veronica Jean, I don't know what has gotten into you."

"A little dope. Lot of beer."

That got her attention.

"Excuse me?" Mom said, her voice going all tight and quiet like it does right before she explodes.

I was in a mood, so I cocked my head and stared right back. Of course, the beer and joint helped with said mood, but I went with it anyway. "What part didn't you hear? Do you need me to repeat it?"

That was over the top, even for me, and I could tell Mom wasn't sure how to react. I also thought I had given her a stroke, what with her face going all purple and everything. I wanted a drink of beer, but thought better of it as I continued to watch Mom.

It took several seconds of breathing deeply through her nose before Mom spoke again. "I would think you'd want better for yourself, Veronica."

That did it. Between the snarky comment by Miss Priss at school, and now my own mother, I snapped. I eyed her waitress uniform up and down slowly. "You mean, better than serving the local slop down at the feeding hole?"

Mom's face instantly went white, and I didn't blame her. It was a low blow, and I felt horrible, even through the haze of pot and beer clouding my mind.

Her voice trembled. "I work very hard-"

"I know you do, Mom," I said, tapping the bottom of the beer bottle on the arm of the chair. My tone was off-hand, but I really did know how hard she worked. After Dad left, it was all she could do to make ends meet.

Suddenly, Mom deflated, her shoulders sinking down and forward. She pressed a shaking hand over her eyes and took a deep breath. Finally, she dropped her hand and looked at me, and for the first time I thought about how old she looked. When had her hair started to go gray? When had lines begun creasing the edges of her eyes?

"Do you think I want this for you, Veronica?" She swept her hand in an arc, taking in the rundown, ragged trailer. "I'm doing the best I can on my own!"

"I don't want money," I said, my voice barely above a whisper.

"What?"

"I said, 'I don't want money,'" I snapped, my anger surging full force.

"Why not?" Mom looked honestly confused.

"I've seen what it does to people." I raised the beer to my lips, regardless of my mother's glare, and pushed images of Emma Swann out of my mind.

"You need to finish school, get a decent job that will support you, whether you get rich or not."

"That's not going to happen." I downed the rest of the beer and prayed for the buzz to take over. I really did not want to have this conversation.

"Yes. It. Is." Mom's hands landed on her hips, and I fought the urge to laugh.

"No. It's. Not." I glared right back. "Didn't you know? I just got word from the school – I'm not graduating, Mom."

For the second time, Mom's face paled as my words sank in. "What?" she whispered.

I slammed the bottle down on the rickety table beside me. "No matter how hard I work, I can't graduate. So how's that for your golden plans?" I sneered.

Mom must have missed my tone, because her eyes were distant, her mind obviously working overtime. "I'll call the principal tomorrow-"

"No." It came out flat and hard.

Mom's eyes narrowed. "You are a minor, Veronica Jean, and you *will* attend school, and we *will* find a way for you to graduate. At worst there are online options to help you get your diploma."

I laughed, my voice rough. "I'm not doing summer school, Mom. In a classroom *or* on a computer."

Mom's eyebrows rose. "You don't have a choice."

Suddenly I rocketed to my feet, my eyes narrowing. "You going to turn me in to the cops if I don't go to school, *Mom?*" My tone was scathing, and I could see it hurt, deep in her eyes, but I didn't care. My hurt overrode hers. "It's *your* weed I've been smoking, Mom, *your* beer. You've been supplying to a minor. Won't the cops love to hear that?"

Mom's breath sucked in harshly. "You wouldn't."

Would I? At that exact moment, I didn't know. "Try me," I said instead.

"I haven't given you permission to use those things!"

"You haven't tried to stop me, either. Come on, Mom. Like you didn't wonder why your stash got smaller so fast?"

The guilty look on her face was all I needed. I had won.

"I'm not going to school tomorrow. There's no point."

I stalked past Mom and headed for my room. It was silent behind me. The door to my room slammed harder than I expected, and I winced. I don't know why I felt so bad. School was out; I didn't have to go any longer. I hated it anyway. I won.

So why did it feel like a huge vacuum had just opened up in my chest?

Wallace

12.

I paused outside Room 5, staring at the tarnished metal placard on the wall next to the door. Once upon a time, I used to like sociology. Until this stupid project. Sighing, I pulled the door open and walked into the classroom.

The first thing I noticed was that Veronica wasn't there. The second was that Emma sat in her usual seat beside the "cool kids." I passed her without comment and settled into my own seat. I shouldn't have worried; she didn't even look up from her all-important conversation.

Much too soon for my comfort, Ms. Hawthorne took attendance and told us to split into our groups. I stayed where I was and hoped Emma Swann would forget about my existence. No such luck.

The chair next to mine creaked as she settled into it, and I stayed hunched over my notebook, waiting for the overexuberant greeting. Except it never came. I peeked at her out of the corner of my eye. Emma sat with her notebook on the desk in front of her, closed. She stared at it with a distant look in her eyes.

This was exactly the type of thing I hated. Now what was I supposed to do? I definitely didn't want to ask her what was wrong;

sorry, I just didn't care that much. But I could hear both Abuela's and Mamá's voices in my head, scolding me for being rude.

Sighing, I straightened up and glanced over. "Everything okay?"

Emma blinked, then turned her gaze toward me. "Huh? Oh…uh, yeah."

Well, that was convincing. But who was I to question her further and accuse her of lying? We barely knew each other. Down to business then.

"Are we still using my family for the project?"

Emma blinked rapidly, and I began to wonder if there was something in her eye. Then she sat up a little straighter and flipped her notebook open as if she hadn't just been staring a hole into it seconds earlier.

"Yeah. I made some notes yesterday. Things we should talk to your parents about. It would be awesome to talk to your brothers and sisters too. I mean, if you have any," she added hastily, looking mortified that she might have said something to offend me.

I felt myself soften toward her a little. Sure, Emma was kind of annoying, and wasn't always that nice, but she didn't seem *that* bad. Veronica would have said something ten times worse and not been sorry at all. Speaking of Veronica…

"Where is Veronica?" I asked abruptly, looking around the room and not seeing her black hair or blue nails anywhere.

Emma's eyes darkened so suddenly, I caught myself staring. "Who cares?" she snapped stiffly, flipping a page in her notebook so fast it ripped halfway up from the bottom.

What the-

Maybe I didn't want to know. Veronica definitely wasn't nice to me, so maybe she and Emma had gotten into it as well. I felt myself soften a little more toward Emma.

"Um, I have two brothers and two sisters."

Emma looked up, the relief on her face making me uncomfortable enough that I looked back at my notebook.

"Are they younger or older than you?" she asked quietly.

"Younger. I'm the oldest."

"I have a younger sister."

We looked at each other, and I dropped my eyes quickly. As a rule, I didn't talk to girls much, so I had no idea what to say next. I heard paper rustling as Emma looked through her notes.

"Um, were you born here?" she asked hesitantly.

"No, we moved to Texas when I was five, and to Michigan when I was eight. And we can't keep doing this." I was somewhere between annoyed and frustrated, making me lose some of the shyness factor.

Emma's pen halted mid-word. "What?"

I rubbed my hand down my face. "You can't keep thinking I'm going to bite your head off with every question you ask."

"You did yesterday." Her voice matched mine for irritation, and it stopped me short.

"I'm just – I'm just not used to talking about my family, okay? We don't really – we're just private, I guess."

Emma paused. "We can choose a different subject for the project," she finally said, but I could tell that was the last thing she wanted.

"Like what?" I snapped.

I expected Emma to yell back at me, but instead she clutched her pen tighter and turned her face away from me. Now I felt really bad, and I could hear Mamá and Abuela screaming at me in my head.

"Look, it's fine," I sighed. Glancing sideways at her, I said, "Besides, we wouldn't want to miss all of Veronica's scathing comments that we know she's been working on, would we?"

Emma's face snapped up to mine, her eyes wide. Then she started to laugh. I offered a crooked smile, feeling good that I had lightened the mood a little. Until I looked up and saw Emma's friends looking over at us with narrowed eyes. Emma must have seen it too, because her laughter cut off abruptly, and she buried her nose back in her notes. Clenching my jaw, I looked back down at my own papers, tracing my most recent doodle, a gazebo.

"So, um, what was it like living in Mexico?"

I tried to get my mind back on track. "It's…different."

Emma squinted at me. "Okay…I need a little more than that."

Squeezing my eyes shut for a minute, I thought about how I could make this girl who had everything understand.

"There are some parts of Mexico that have a lot of money, and some that don't. There are villages of squatters that have no electricity, running water, or Internet, and their floors are made of dirt."

Emma looked horrified. "Did you have to live in one of those villages?"

I wondered if she was thinking about what life would be like without her phone. "Not at first." I fell silent. I really, *really* didn't like talking about my life. A touch on my arm startled me, and I looked up to find Emma's face bright red as she quickly took her hand off my arm.

"Um, can you tell me what happened, Wallace?" she asked, and bent over her notebook, scribbling who knew what.

I couldn't see any way around it. "My dad works construction here, but he also did in Mexico. The work industry is very different there than it is here, though."

Emma stopped doodling and leaned over her desk, her expression showing interest. "What do you mean?"

I shrugged. "In the U.S., people know how much something is going to cost. When they want something built, they get bids from lots of contractors, then choose the one that fits with their budget."

Glancing at Emma, I noticed her attention hadn't waivered, so I continued. "In Mexico, if someone wants something built, they just hire someone and start. They have no idea of what the real cost will be, so a lot of them run out of money before the project is even done."

"Then what happens?"

I shrugged again. "It just sits, half done. Most are abandoned and never gone back to at all."

Emma's eyes narrowed. "But...but that seems so...I don't get it," she finally finished. "Why don't they price it out and get bids then? If that keeps happening, why wouldn't they make sure it would work before starting?"

"A different culture, a different way of thinking, I guess."

Quiet for a moment, Emma finally looked back at me. "Does that have something to do with your dad?"

Right. I had forgotten where I was going with that. "Yeah. When the owners of the property ran out of money, it meant the contractors were out of a job. You never knew when another one would pop up, or how long it would last."

"That had to be hard." Emma's gaze was distant again, and I wondered what she was thinking about.

"Yeah. Well, eventually we ran out of money and ended up in one of the squatter villages because we didn't have anywhere else we could afford to go."

"Is…is that why you moved to the United States?"

I nodded. "From what I've pieced together from conversations I've overheard during the years, yeah. My parents don't talk about that much with us kids."

Emma's pen moved across the page, her loopy handwriting covering several lines before her hand slowed. Finally, she looked up at me. "I'm sorry, Wallace. I – I never had it that bad, and I can't imagine-"

The bell cut her off, and I figured that was a good thing. Anger was building in my chest. I didn't want her pity. I didn't need it; my family and I had a good life, and we were all together. We didn't need money like some people.

"Hey, can we meet at your house this weekend? To talk about some of this with your family?"

I wanted to yell no, but nodded instead. Just what I wanted to do on a weekend. Not that I had any awesome social plans, but this was so much worse. "Sure."

"If you see Veronica, why don't you tell her where and when? Oh, and here's my phone number." Emma ripped off the corner of a piece of paper and scribbled a line of numbers. "Text me your address and what works for you guys, okay? I have a party tonight, but am free the rest of the weekend." She shoved the paper toward me.

I didn't have time to answer before she bolted to her feet and ran to catch up with the other popular kids. Lockers slammed and kids shouted in the hall, but it all seemed far away. Doing this sociology project about my family had to be the stupidest thing I had ever done. Now I had to have rich-girl Emma and goth-girl Veronica over to my house? And actually let them talk to my family?

There were so many ways I could see this ending, and none of them were good.

Emma

13.

I didn't want to go home. I had to, though, because Hailee was there. No way was I going to leave her alone with Mom right now. Besides, Ian was going to pick me up for the party.

Dad tried texting several times during school, but I ignored them all. I didn't know what to say to him, anyway. He cheated on my mom – on all of us. How could he do something that would tear apart our family like that? I felt sick to my stomach every time I thought about it, and talking about it with Dad didn't sound fun. At all.

My heart sank when I saw Mom's car in the garage. I'm not sure why I thought she might not be home; she was always home now that we had money. The day after the first check with lots of zeros was deposited in the bank, she walked out of her pharmacy job downtown and never looked back. She started looking at wine bottles instead.

I inched through the mudroom door, trying not to make any noise, and could immediately hear the television blaring. A soap opera, always Mom's favorite. I didn't stop to see if she had the usual glass of wine glued to her hand before jogging lightly up the steps.

Hailee was in her room, headphones on, foot tapping to the beat of whatever she was listening to as her eyes skimmed the book in her hands. I tapped her bopping foot to get her attention.

"Hey, sis. Listen, do you have a friend you can stay with tonight?"

Hailee pulled the headphones down so they curled around her neck. "What?"

"A friend," I repeated impatiently. "Do you have a friend you can stay with tonight?"

Her forehead scrunched into furrows. "Why?"

"I have a party tonight and I'm pretty sure you don't want to hang with Mom all by yourself." I picked up Hailee's duffle bag and looked at her over my shoulder. "Am I right?"

Hailee scrambled off the bed. "I can stay at Stacy's house. She asked me earlier, but I didn't think Mom would let me."

"Sometimes it's easier to ask forgiveness then permission," I muttered as I watched my little sister toss stuff in her bag.

Hailee paused. "What?" She looked confused.

"Nothing. I'll take you over there as soon as you're done."

Once Hailee was packed, we snuck down the stairs and out to my car. It was quiet for the first couple of minutes. Then Hailee checked her phone.

"I have a text from Dad." She looked over at me. "Did he text you today?"

I nodded. "Yeah. A few times."

Hailee looked back at her phone, but her fingers remained still. "I don't know what to say to him," she said quietly.

I glanced at her, then back at the road. "Don't worry about it now. We can figure that out later. Together," I added, hoping that would help her to not worry so much.

Hailee didn't say anything, but I saw her slide the phone back into the pocket of her bag. It was a short ride to Stacy's house, and I ruffled Hailee's hair and gave her a smile I didn't feel as she got out of the car. Back at home, I tiptoed through the mudroom, but this time I wasn't so lucky.

"Emma! Glad you're home. I'm making lasagna for dinner."

Mom stood at the kitchen counter, stirring the contents of a large bowl. Giving the wooden spoon a vigorous swipe around the bowl, a large glob of cheese and spices shot out and onto the counter. Swearing, she scooped it up with her hands and plopped it back into the bowl. Looking up to see me staring, she giggled and pointed a finger at me.

"Don't ever swear, you hear me?" Then she giggled again and winked before picking up the ever-present glass of wine next to the bowl.

I rolled my eyes. "Sure."

"Anyway," Mom continued, setting down the wine glass so hard I thought it would break, "it will be nice to all eat together, don't you think?"

"Gee, Mom," I hedged. "Hailee is at Stacy's for the night, and I have a party at Ben's house. Ian said he would pick me up in just a little bit."

The spoon landed hard in the bowl, and Mom glared at me. "Well, it would have been nice to know that before I went to all this trouble," she snapped.

I refrained from mentioning that the only thing she had in the bowl was cottage cheese and some spices. There were no noodles cooked, or within sight, no meat ready, and the oven wasn't even on.

"And who gave Hailee permission to have a sleepover with a friend, anyway?" Mom was really ramping up, starting to pace back and forth behind the counter. "I never talked to her mother." She paused. "At least, I don't think I did."

Straightening my shoulders, I sucked in my breath and took one for the team. "I told Hailee that she could. I took her over just a few minutes ago."

Mom whirled around, her expression livid. "I am the mother in this house, do you understand, Emma Ann? You were out of line."

My eyes narrowed slightly. A feeling of sadness washed through me suddenly, and I almost staggered from it, it was so unexpected. I wanted to yell at her to start *acting* like our mother then, but knew I couldn't. She was already drunk, and would only get more furious.

Truth was...I missed my mom. Not this woman who could barely stand up straight, but the woman who used to tuck me in at night after asking how my day had gone. My real mom wouldn't have let me go to the party at Ben's house before calling Ben's parents, and most of the other parents of kids who would be there, to make sure it would be properly supervised.

Feeling like I might start crying, I gave a small shrug and muttered "Sorry" under my breath. Then I turned toward the stairs, praying that Ian would decide to show up early. I had every intention of hiding in my room until he got here.

I tried to write while I waited, but my thoughts were scattered and incoherent, and my pen only tapped on the page, making small black dots over and over again. Finally, I heard a car pull into the driveway, and I grabbed my jacket and bolted for the door before Mom could manage to roll herself off the couch.

"See you, Mom!" I called as I burst out the front door. I almost ran over a very surprised Ian who had begun walking up the front path.

"Um, hi, Emma," he said as I raced up to him.

"Hi," I responded breathlessly, then grabbed his arm and yanked him back toward his car. "I'm ready to go, are you ready to go? Great."

I was in the passenger seat with the door closed before Ian even opened the driver's side door. As Ian slid into his seat, I kept an eye on the front door to make sure my mother didn't make an appearance.

"Is everything okay?" Ian asked, as he turned the key in the ignition.

My face flushed with embarrassment. I had been so intent on getting out of the house, I hadn't stopped to think about what my actions would look like to him. There was no way I was going to admit how dysfunctional our family was though.

"Yeah, great." I gave a shaky laugh. "Just ready for a night out, you know? To relax a little."

Ian grinned. "Me too."

It was easy to talk to Ian. I don't think I realized how easy until we were actually alone together and the conversation wasn't dominated by Sami, Tiffany, and Ben. Ian and I both tended to be a bit more on the quiet side when we were together as a group.

Ian told me about how his dog stole the chicken off the table during dinner a few weeks ago, and I laughed so hard my sides ached. It had been a long time since I really laughed.

There were so many kids at Ben's house that we had to park way down the winding drive and walk up to the house. It was a huge house, all glass and concrete. I personally hated it – it looked more like a modern office building than a home to me. Music pounded loud enough to hear outside as we walked up, and Ian and I exchanged a quick look and a shrug before he opened the front door for me.

The music was so loud Ian had to shout in my ear that he would find a place for our coats before I heard him. As soon as he disappeared, a red Solo cup of beer was shoved into my hand by a kid I didn't even know.

The foamy liquid sloshed over the side and coated my hand. I could count the number of times I had had alcohol on one hand. Beer made me feel buzzed fast. Ben called me a lightweight. I hated how I didn't feel in control, so I usually didn't drink. Tonight, however…the tension in my shoulders made me feel desperate for a release.

By the time Ian found me on the dance floor, I was on my second Solo cup, and I felt like I didn't have a care in the world. Screw Mom and Dad. Screw Veronica and the stupid sociology project. Screw everything – I was ready to have *fun*.

Ian's hands found my waist as we moved to the music, and he leaned forward to yell a joke in my ear. I threw my head back and laughed, feeling better than I had in a long time. He leaned toward me again and yelled, "It's great to see you smile." At least, I think that's what he said. The beer and the pounding music were making my mind jittery, and everything felt disconnected.

Sami and Tiffany danced up to us, both whooping and hollering, their own red cups in hand. I still hadn't seen Ben, and it was safe to assume his parents were nowhere nearby. Another Solo cup was pushed into my hand, then another, and I lost count as to how many beers I had. I didn't care.

Ian spun me around and pulled me against him, his laughter ringing in my ears. The ringing didn't go away when he let go again, and I stumbled as Tiffany bumped into me from behind. The whole room tilted at a crazy angle, and my stomach with it. Suddenly, I remembered the other reason why I didn't drink.

Crap. This wasn't good.

I staggered and lurched my way through the crowd, my lips pressed tightly together in an effort to keep the beer from making a sudden reappearance. I finally made it to the hallway. The first door I tried was a library; I left the door open as I stumbled to the next door. That one revealed Sami and some guy I didn't know kissing on a bed.

Finally. The door to the bathroom slammed against the wall as I toppled through. I barely got the lid of the toilet up before the beer came back with a vengeance. My stomach heaved and heaved – so many times I thought I might be sick again just from the horrible wrenching motions.

When it finally seemed I didn't have anything left to throw up, I leaned back against the wall, closing my eyes against the spinning ceiling. Groaning, I wiped the back of my hand over my soiled mouth and turned my gaze toward the door where the last person on earth I wanted to see stood staring at me with a smirk on her face.

Veronica

14.

Well, well, well. Miss Priss in all her glory, hunched against her porcelain throne.

I leaned against the doorframe, beer in one hand, smoking cigarette in the other. I lifted the cigarette to my mouth as I contemplated all the fun I could have with this little scenario.

Priss groaned and shifted against the wall. What was her real name? Suddenly, I couldn't even remember. My lip curled as she groaned again, then lunged for the toilet just before her stomach relieved itself once more. Her hair was plastered to her head, sweat soaking through her clothes. I glanced around the hall, but didn't see anyone coming to claim the Priss.

Looking back into the bathroom, I switched my cigarette to the hand holding the beer, then pulled my phone from my jeans pocket. This really was too good to pass up. Who knew when it would come in handy? I snapped a couple of pictures, then shoved the phone back into my pocket.

Priss' eyes rolled back in her head, and she slid to the floor, her blonde hair pooling on the tile. I took a couple more hits of the beer and the cigarette, then sighed and stepped into the room, flicking the cigarette into the vomit-filled toilet bowl. As much as I didn't like it, I had been in Priss' situation before, and it looked like she had had way too much. Which meant she shouldn't be alone.

Setting my Solo cup on the counter, I crouched down and nudged Priss' shoulder, my lip curling as I got a good whiff of what a rich girl smelled like after a vomit fest.

"Hey."

Priss just groaned, her eyes half shut.

"Hey. Priss. Who'd you come here with?"

Nothing.

"Come on, I don't have all night. I crashed this party and haven't even had the chance to get drunk yet. Who're you with?"

"Eeenn."

I squinted and leaned closer, then immediately leaned back after catching another hint of her breath. "Who?" *Seriously, this isn't rocket science, Priss.*

"Eeee-uuuuu."

I ran a hand down my face in frustration. This was really the last thing I wanted to deal with tonight. The whole purpose of crashing the party was so I could get wasted on free beer and forget about life for awhile. I looked back at Priss' clumped hair lying over her face and exhaled loudly. I could leave her here. Really. I didn't come with her. She wasn't my responsibility.

A noise at the door made me look up. A boy I only recognized by sight, but knew was a jerk of the third degree, leered at me. "Hey, lookin' for a good time?" he slurred.

My eyes narrowed. "Get lost, before I decide this isn't one of my nice days."

Extending his middle finger, the boy lurched away from the door and disappeared. His presence, however, was the deciding factor. Leaving Priss here wasn't an option. Not with jerks like that around who were looking for anything wearing a skirt. I'd had too much experience with that as well.

Sighing, I grabbed Priss' arm and got to my feet, trying to pull her into a sitting position. "Come on, Priss, let's get you home." Although how I would do that when she couldn't even tell me the name of the person she was with, much less her address, I didn't know.

"No!"

Well, that had her lucid. At least for a second. "What?" I snapped, my patience already nonexistent. Her resistance wasn't helping.

When she didn't say anything else, I grabbed her other arm and pulled hard, grunting with the effort. Finally, she was in a...somewhat upright position. "All right," I wheezed. "Let's try this again. You need to help me; I can't carry you home."

Priss jerked away from me with some sort of hidden strength. My hands slid off her arms, and she flopped backward onto the rug in front of the sink. "No!" she yelled at the ceiling, her eyes glazed.

Hands on my hips, I glared at her. "Listen, Priss, I'm about to leave you here. I don't need this crap, so get it together and help me get you home."

To my surprise, Priss' head lolled toward me, her eyes suddenly clear, and she whispered, "Not home."

She blinked, and the glazed look came back. I continued to stand over her, my emotions rolling like waves in a storm. One part of me wanted to walk away and let whatever happened to her happen. The other part related to the desperation in the girl at my feet when she thought she would be forced to go home.

Was it possible that not everything was perfect in Rich Land? Why didn't Priss want to go home?

Breathing hard through my nose, I knew what I had to do. I just didn't *want* to do it. I crouched down until I could look directly into her eyes.

"Hey. Priss." I snapped my fingers in front of her face until I was fairly sure I had at least a small amount of awareness. "You wanna come home with me?"

Priss looked back at me, and I was surprised to see tears in her eyes. One leaked out and rolled down her temple into her hair. Crap. I didn't need tears too.

More to avoid having to look in her eyes than because of a desire to help, I reached out and hooked my hands under her armpits. "Come on, Priss. Help a person out, huh?"

She finally seemed to come out of her stupor long enough to help push herself to her feet. Then she swayed, her face turning ashen and her lips pressing together so hard they looked bloodless.

"Don't even think about hurling again, Priss," I warned her. "So help me, I will leave you here."

Priss swallowed hard, then tightened her arm around my neck. I kept one hand on the wrist hanging off my shoulder, and put the other arm around her waist, fisting my hand in her shirt in case she decided to keel over. We stumbled toward the door, both of us breathing hard, but for different reasons.

I don't think either one of us realized how loud the party had become until we left the bathroom and were assaulted by pounding music and the yells of classmates as they started to do shots off each others' stomachs. Priss' head lolled forward, and suddenly I was holding her up more than she was walking. Crap. Had she passed out?

Half walking and half dragging Priss through the crowd, I shoved my way toward the wall and began to follow it until I came to a set of patio doors. They were flung open, and the cool spring air instantly dissolved in the heat of the moving bodies inside. I pushed past a guy and girl making out and hauled Priss out onto the stone pathway.

Once we were a ways from the house, the cool air actually felt cool, and it seemed to revive Priss a little. At least she started moving her feet again. Which was good, because my car was on the other side of the house and down the hill.

I had no idea how we managed to make it to the car, but I finally saw it through the darkness and heaved Priss up to the side of the passenger door, pinning her there with my hip while I fished my keys out of my pocket. The cool air slithered through my sweat-soaked shirt, and I shivered. Priss started to slide just as I hit the unlock button on the key fob, and I planted my free hand in the middle of her chest and pinned her back to the car.

It took a fair amount of wrestling to get the door open and Priss inside, but it only involved a lot of swearing on my part and one lost shoe on Priss' part, and she was inside. Breathing heavily, I snatched her shoe off the ground and tossed it in her lap before slamming the door. What had possibly possessed me to think it was a good idea to bring this snotty rich kid home? I started the car before I carried through with my thought of dumping her on the ground and taking off.

The ride back to my house was fairly quiet. Until Priss started snoring. I swear, that girl could rival a chainsaw. Rolling my eyes, I shoved my elbow in her side. That got her to quit – for all of two seconds. Grinding my teeth, I did my best to tune out the horrendous noise.

Mom's car was in the driveway when I pulled up to the trailer. Double crap. How was I going to explain this?

Grunting, I hauled Priss from the car and draped her arm over my shoulder. We both almost went down when Priss caught a foot on the broken step, but I managed to keep us upright. I could see old Mrs. Wilson peering through her curtains again. I couldn't flip her off, so I settled for the nastiest look I could muster while sweating profusely and lugging a half-conscious drunk girl.

The door slammed against the wall as we stumbled through, and *my* foot caught this time, propelling us both forward. I barely managed to swing us toward the couch before we went down. Priss' upper body landed on the couch, and I landed on her legs where they splayed on the floor. Somehow I managed to crack my elbow on the coffee table, and I groaned in pain.

When the throbbing finally died down, I shoved off of Priss' legs and stood up. Looking down, I realized Priss was asleep, her mouth hanging open. "Oh for the love of-" I muttered, then reached down, grabbed her legs, and threw them up onto the couch. Turning, I wanted nothing more than to climb into my own bed, but came face to face with my mother instead.

Her arms crossed, Mom looked at me, one eyebrow arching toward her hairline. "And this is...?" she asked, directing her gaze toward Priss before turning her glare back on me.

Pushing my hair back out of my face, I shrugged as nonchalantly as I could. "A friend." I almost choked on the word and covered it with a cough. "She wanted to stay overnight." Mom obviously didn't believe me, but I pushed past her before she could respond. "Night." I closed my bedroom door firmly behind me.

Mom's sigh was so loud I heard it through the door. I waited until I heard her footsteps stomp back toward her bedroom, then sagged against the door. Now that the battle to get Priss here was done, the nagging feeling I had tried to ignore came back full force. I looked at the door over my shoulder as my thoughts whirled.

Why didn't Priss want to go home?

Wallace
15.

I swung little Gabby up into my arms as she launched a spit bubble at my face. "Mi hermana," I groaned, swiping at my face with my sleeve. "Gabbers, you gotta quit doing that!"

Gabby squealed and clapped her hands, narrowly missing my nose. Rolling my eyes, I plopped her into her high chair, then tousled her hair before going to help Mamá and Abuela put the food on the table. We were eating a lot later than usual because Papá had to work late. My stomach growled as I grabbed a plate of fish in one hand and a plate of soft taco shells in the other, careful to set them well out of little Gabby's reach.

Mamá shuffled around the kitchen silently, though the salsa music playing on the small kitchen radio had her dancing a small step or two as she made the last minute preparations. As I went back for the beans and rice, I caught Abuela's gaze. She narrowed her eyes and then looked toward Mamá. I couldn't get anything past her.

Sighing, I set the bowls down on the table and moved a fork out of Gabby's chubby reach. "Um, Mamá?" I began hesitantly, not sure how to broach the subject I had been thinking about non-stop.

"Si, hijo?" She handed me a stack of plates and turned back toward the stove.

I began setting out the plates while Lucas ran into the room, making rocket noises and zooming a space ship through the air. As he ran back toward the living room, I snatched a napkin out of Gabby's sticky grasp.

"I was wondering…it's been a couple of days…have you had a chance to talk with Papá about the college?"

I saw Mamá's hand hesitate for just a second, then she continued rattling pots on the stove. "Not yet, hijo. Papá has been busy with work."

"I know, Mamá, but-"

A pot slammed down hard as she moved it from the stove to the sink. "Sometimes you need to be more patient, hijo!" Mamá snapped, her back still to me.

I stared at her, shocked. Mamá almost never raised her voice, and I hadn't done anything wrong. I was just *asking*. My eyes darted to Abuela, but she was suddenly very busy wiping down the counter.

"Mamá -"

"Wallace, you must wait! And do not bring it up at dinner, do you hear me? Your Papá needs some time to rest."

"But, Mamá, the deadline-"

"Enough." Mamá's voice was suddenly very quiet and level. All of us knew what that meant. Back off.

My jaw clenched, and I felt my teeth grind together painfully.

A scuffling sound at the back door let us know Papá was home, and he opened the screen and stepped inside, having left his work boots on the back steps. "Hola, familia," he said, his voice light, but his face lined with exhaustion. Papá stepped to the stove and kissed the cheek Mamá raised for him, then put an arm around Abuela's shoulders in a quick hug.

"Wallace, hijo. How was your day?"

My gaze darted to where Mamá glared at me across the room, and Gabby squealed behind me. I heard a utensil hit the floor. In an attempt to avoid answering the question, I dove for the spoon and turned to give it back to Gabby. When I turned back, Papá had gone into the bathroom to do a quick wash up before dinner.

"Wallace, please get your brothers and sister for dinner," Abuela said quietly. Her eyes were sympathetic as she looked at me.

Ten minutes later, we were all seated closely around the table, arms and shoulders jammed together in an effort to all fit in the small space. There was barely enough room for the food, much less our plates.

"God bless this food…" Papá's tired voice recited the brief prayer, and then hands reached toward the food hungrily.

I made sure Lucas and Mateo had what they needed on either side of me while Mamá cut up food for Gabby. Papá was already shoveling in his second taco before I even put together my first. Theresa chattered about the math test she was *sure* she had aced today, and could she go to a sleepover at Sonya's house tomorrow night, Mamá?

Mamá agreed, then there were a few moments of silence while we all ate. Abuela's gaze caught mine as I raised another taco dripping with salsa to my lips, and I knew she had something up her sleeve.

"Wallace, nieto, have you told tu padres, your parents, about the project you are working on for escuela?

My food hovered in front of my mouth as I froze, my eyes murderous as I glared at my beloved abuela. How did she know? How did Abuela know I told Emma and Veronica we could do the sociology project on my family?

"Um, *no*," I said meaningfully, my gaze pointed.

Abuela smiled at me serenely. "Why don't you tell them about it?"

"What project is this, hijo?" Papá asked, wiping his hands on a napkin before reaching for more rice.

Mamá looked at me with interest, and I felt my chest tighten as I placed my taco back on my plate. I looked at it longingly.

"Well, um, we have a sociology project due in a few weeks. I'm, uh, in a group with a couple other kids."

"Bueno, bueno," Papá said, nodding as he mixed beans in with his rice.

Whatever.

Mamá's eyes lit up. "Who are your work partners? Friends, sí?"

"Not really," I said slowly. Abuela continued to smile calmly, even while chewing her food.

Mamá looked confused, but then seemed to brush it aside in her mind. "What is this project about, hijo?"

I rubbed my hands down the legs of my jeans under the table. They suddenly felt incredibly sweaty. "Um, about our family," I mumbled, then shoved half the taco on my plate into my mouth so I wouldn't have to say any more.

Papá's hands stilled over his plate, and Mamá dropped the plastic spoon, scattering rice across the table. Abuela calmly popped a piece of fish into her mouth and chewed slowly.

Mateo, Lucas, and Gabby were oblivious to our parent's reactions, but Theresa glanced at me, her forehead creased with confusion. I gave a half shrug and continued chewing my mouthful of food furiously.

Papá's eyes darkened as he leaned forward over his plate. "What do you mean, about our familia?" His voice was steady, but his brown eyes were harder than I had ever seen them.

I swallowed hard, then glanced at Mamá. She stared at me with a horrified expression, her features twisted into a mask of pain and uncertainty. What was going on?

"Well," I cleared my throat, suddenly feeling like it was hard to speak. "Uh, Emma and Veronica were hoping that we could interview you guys about life in Mexico versus life in the States. You know, the differences in how we live, what is available to us, stuff like that. We also have to conduct interviews with everyone in the family."

Mamá's breath sucked in harshly, her dark skin suddenly looking much lighter. Papá's hands curled into fists beside his plate, then released, then curled again. I felt a flash of fear, though I didn't know why. I knew why *I* didn't want to do the project on my family – I hated any kind of attention at school. Usually it wasn't good. But why would my parents care so much?

"No." Papá's voice was heavy, his dark eyebrows pulled down low.

I gaped at him. "No?"

Papá shook his head. "No. You will not be doing this project on our family."

"But – but, Papá! It's too late to find another subject now! We won't have time to get everything done if we don't start now."

Papá's hands slammed down on the table. Bowls and plates jumped and clattered, and even Gabby's babbles went silent.

"You will find another subject, Wallace! Do you understand me? Our familia is off limits!" He shoved his chair away from the table and stormed out the screen door into the night, his socks making a rough scratching sound on the wooden steps to the yard.

Maybe it was the fact that I still hadn't gotten a good answer on why I couldn't go to the college I wanted, or maybe it was because I was already stressed out from having to deal with Emma and Veronica about this project at school. But anger suddenly took over, and I shoved my own chair back from the table. Throwing my napkin on the table, I followed my father.

"Hijo!"

"Wallace!"

I ignored both Mamá and Abuela and barreled through the screen door and out onto the back lawn. Papa's shadow was near the back fence. He paced back and forth, back and forth. "Go back inside, Wallace."

"No." I stopped a few feet away and folded my arms stubbornly. "I want to know what is going on."

Papá's eyes flashed in the light spilling from the kitchen windows as he turned to glare at me. "It is not your choice, hijo. You need to leave it alone. Ahora!"

Something inside me snapped at his refusal to tell me why he was so angry. "I'm not going back inside until I know why we can't do the project about our family!" I shouted.

Papá was suddenly right in front of me, and it was all I could do not to back up when he turned his dark gaze on me. "There are things you don't know, Wallace," he said, his voice dangerously low. "I can't let you do this project because it could put our family in danger."

I inhaled harshly, my eyes wide. "What-"

Papá shook his head. "Find another project, hijo." He brushed past me back into the house.

I stared after him, confused, and now a little afraid. What had just happened?

Emma

16.

I hadn't even opened my eyes yet and I already wanted to die.

My head pounded to the beat of an invisible drummer, my throat was raw, and my stomach felt so queasy I didn't want to move for fear of what might happen.

"Morning, sunshine!"

My whole body jerked in surprise, and I instantly regretted the movement as my head threatened to burst and my stomach rolled violently. Groaning, I threw a hand up over my eyes and split my fingers apart so I could peek through them. Veronica was slouched in a threadbare, overstuffed chair, a cigarette dangling from her fingers.

"What the-" I immediately scrambled to a sitting position, then immediately leaned forward with my head in my hands, trying to get the drummer in my head and the swimmer in my stomach to settle down. After several seconds, I was able to raise my head enough to look up at Veronica. She grinned.

"How ya feeling, Priss? Want something to eat? A walk in the sunshine? Maybe some beer?"

I glared at her, each suggestion making my body revolt even more. "What happened? Why am I here?" And where was *here*?

Veronica took a slow drag off her cigarette and let the smoke drift out of her mouth, staring at me the whole time. It took everything I had not to curl my lip in disgust. I never understood why people thought smoking was cool.

"You were puking in a bathroom, gorgeous. Real attractive. Sweaty hair, the whole thing." Veronica rolled her hand in the air, cigarette smoke making a transparent 'o' in the space between us. "I asked who you were with, but you couldn't tell me. You know. In your condition." She grinned.

I hated her. I really hated her at that moment.

"You kind of freaked out when I said I was going to take you home."

Veronica paused, and I felt my face heat. I looked away, horrified at what else I might have revealed.

"Relax, Priss."

My eyes shot back to Veronica, surprised at the lack of venom in her voice. It almost seemed like she cared or something.

"I brought you home with me, and ta-da – " she waved her hand in the air again. "Here we are. You look great, by the way." She smirked.

I knew the "caring" in her voice was too good to last.

My gaze suddenly fell on my phone. It sat on a cracked and scratched coffee table in front of the couch. My stomach churned even more as I realized what my mom must be thinking. And Ian! Ignoring Veronica, I pressed a hand to my pounding forehead and thumbed my phone active with my other.

"I already answered their texts."

"What?"

Veronica shifted, throwing a leg over the arm of the chair. "I saw the texts from your mom and some guy named Ian. You don't have a passcode on your phone, so I just pretended to be you and said you decided to stay at a friend's house." She rolled her eyes on the last word, but she also looked vaguely uncomfortable.

"Thanks," I said quietly, honestly thankful for what she had done. It could have felt like an invasion of privacy, but I was more grateful that I wouldn't be in trouble with Mom and have to answer a bunch of questions about where I had been once I got home.

I glanced around the small room. It was actually a living room and kitchen combination, one leading right into the other. I could see a hallway off to the side of the kitchen, and I figured that was where the bedrooms were. It was a really small space to live. I eyed the furniture, noticing the mismatched pieces and how worn everything looked.

"So…this is your house?" I asked tentatively, not sure what else to say. Veronica and I weren't exactly friends. What do you say to someone who hates you, anyway?

Veronica's eyes darkened. "Yeah," she said in a voice that dared me to make fun of her. "Mom's at work, in case you were hoping to meet her." Sarcasm dripped from the words.

No, I really didn't care to meet Mrs. Bennett. Not if she was anything like her daughter. My gaze landed on an end table with two doors in the front that opened out. An intricate design wound around both sides, though there were scratches in many places, marring the otherwise smooth surface. Eyes lighting up, I forgot about my headache.

"We had one of those!" I said, pointing toward the end table.

"Yeah?" Veronica said again, this time sounding hesitant. It was obvious she couldn't tell if I was mocking her or not.

I felt a grin splitting my face as I remembered storing coloring books in the small alcove behind the two doors, then later hiding the teen magazines my mom told me I couldn't buy when I was twelve.

"Yeah! I used to hide stuff in there I didn't want my mom to find. She never opened it," I explained, though Veronica hadn't asked. My eyes lost some of their light. "We got rid of it in the move. Mom said it didn't fit the style of the new house."

It was quiet for so long, I finally looked over at Veronica. She stared at me with an odd expression on her face, one I couldn't interpret. I flushed, suddenly feeling every pound of my headache again. That, and a very dry mouth.

"Um, could I have a glass of water? Please?" I asked, not sure how Veronica would respond to me right now.

"Sure," she said slowly, then got to her feet and walked the few feet to the kitchen sink.

As the water ran, I slowly got to my feet, testing out not only my stomach, but the rest of my body as well. I felt shaky, and wasn't sure if I could walk well or not, but I was able to take a couple of steps. There were some pictures on another small table near the far wall. I tottered over to it, trying to ignore the cadence in my head from the invisible drummer.

"Here."

"Thanks," I said, absently taking the glass of water Veronica held out to me. I was distracted by the pictures.

It felt like I was staring at a different person. The pictures were of Veronica, I was sure. The eyeliner was there, the dark nail polish...but she was *smiling*. Also a few years younger, I realized as I squinted at the framed pictures.

"Anything interesting?"

The voice was mocking and hard, jarring me out of my musings. With a jolt, I turned to see Veronica still standing next to me, her arms crossed, eyes cold. I felt embarrassed, but something stopped me from walking away. It was something I had seen on the table...

Turning back toward the pictures, I pulled on the edge of a frame that was almost hidden behind another. My breath caught as I saw a grinning Veronica wrapped in the arms of a handsome man, a beautiful woman with dark hair matching Veronica's standing next to them both. The photographer had caught her mid-laugh.

"Is this your family?" I asked, feeling a sense of loss, though I couldn't figure out why.

The frame was snatched from my grasp, and Veronica shoved it down between the arm of the chair she had been sitting in and the seat cushion. "Not anymore," she snapped cryptically.

I was debating whether or not to ask her about it when she started walking toward the door of the small home. "Come on, Priss. It's time you went home."

"Wait."

I don't know why I said it; it certainly wasn't because I enjoyed talking to Veronica. But something inside me told me to wait. Mom used to call it an internal check.

"What?"

Veronica was exasperated, and I couldn't blame her. I stared at her silently, not sure what to say. Why *had* I told her to wait?

"Why weren't you in school yesterday?" I suddenly blurted, surprising myself as much as the girl in front of me.

Veronica recovered quickly, her expression closing off so fast I blinked rapidly three times, not sure what exactly had happened.

"Why?" she asked, her voice flat and void of any emotion.

"Um, because Wallace and I noticed you weren't in sociology class," I responded hesitantly, not sure why she seemed so distant. Wait. Veronica always seemed distant.

"So?"

I shrugged. "We had talked about getting together this weekend, and I thought..."

"Sometimes you think too much, Priss."

That grated. "Stop calling me Priss," I shot back.

Veronica shrugged. "Make me."

I actually thought about it. I actually contemplated throwing myself across the few feet separating us and pounding that awful smirk off her face. But I was also smart enough to know that wouldn't end well. For me. Especially while having a hangover.

Sighing, I threw up my hands in frustration. "Are you willing to get together with us this weekend or not?" I asked, feeling extremely exasperated.

"No." Veronica once again turned toward the door.

"Why not?" Geez, apparently hangovers put me in an argumentative mood.

Veronica turned back toward me slowly, her face a mask of conflicting emotions. Mostly I saw anger and irritation.

"I'm not coming back to school."

"What?" I asked dumbly, not sure what she meant.

"Come on, Priss, turn that blonde brain on for once. I'm quitting school." Veronica swung back toward the door, and this time I followed, almost in a trance.

I didn't know what to say. I had never known anyone who dropped out of school before. And why? Why would she want to drop out of school anyway? I just didn't get it.

"Don't ask me why."

Veronica's warning came right at the moment I opened my mouth to do just that. I quickly snapped it shut and followed her out the door.

The ride to my house was tense and silent. It was almost more unbearable than being at home. Almost. I felt that way until we pulled into my driveway. Then being trapped in a car with Veronica seemed like a vacation.

I turned to tell Veronica thank you, but when I faced her, the hate in her eyes as she stared up at my house made me reach for the door handle instead. I walked up the driveway to the door leading into the mud room, my ears clearly catching the sound of tires squealing as Veronica backed out of the driveway and took off.

As I placed my hand on the door handle and turned it, I had to fight the urge to race after her and beg her to take me with her. I was about to walk into a home that didn't seem like a home. Not mine, anyway.

But it is yours, whether you like it or not, my mind argued as the door swung wide. Sighing, I stepped over the threshold and closed the door behind me.

Veronica

17.

That girl really irritated me. Geez, it felt good to have her gone and to drive out of that ritzy neighborhood.

Rolling up to a stop sign, I checked to make sure no one was behind me, then took out a cigarette. Blowing smoke out of the cracked window, I kept going, still feeling edgy. Finally, I pulled over to the side of the road and took out my phone.

Scrolling through my apps, I found the one for the Star Theatre and checked out what movies were playing that afternoon. I didn't feel like going home, mainly because I didn't feel like being alone.

The new slasher movie everyone was talking about started in forty-five minutes. Perfect. I switched over to contacts and hit Liam's name. He must have been bored, because he picked up after the first ring.

"Hey. Wanna see a movie?"

* * * *

I stretched my legs out in front of me, leaning back on the hard bench as I waited for Liam. The movie theater was a few storefronts down; the bench sat in front of a small coffee shop. Every time someone walked in and out of the shop, the smell of coffee was overpowering, making me want to gag. There wasn't another bench nearby, so I lit a cigarette to cover the coffee smell.

As I waited, the activity at the small hardware store across the narrow street got my attention. A car that had seen better days was parked at the curb. The door to the store opened, and a stocky Hispanic man walked out, pushing a rolling cart loaded with short pieces of wood, boxes of nails, and some other stuff I couldn't figure out from this far away. An old, short Hispanic woman in long, bright-colored skirts shuffled behind him.

The man popped the trunk of the rusted and dented car, then turned and began talking to the old woman. After a couple of seconds, he turned to walk back into the store, leaving the trunk open and the rolling cart next to the woman. She looked from the cart to the trunk while digging one hand into a small bag of candy she clutched tightly.

Taking another drag of my cigarette, I leaned my head back and blew the smoke at the sky, watching the clouds move for a second before tilting my head back up. My whole body jerked in surprise when my eyes met those of the old woman across the street. She didn't look away when she saw me looking at her. Creepy.

Uncomfortable, I looked away, then back again, hoping she had gone back to her candy. Nope. Her eyes drilled into mine from across the street. Finally, she raised one hand and beckoned me to come to her.

What the-?

My head swiveled from side to side, thinking there had to be someone standing close to me that she meant. I glanced back across the street. The old woman was still waving at me to cross. What did she want? To sell me something? I wasn't interested.

"No thanks," I called, then brought my cigarette to my lips and looked away. Out of the corner of my eye, I could see the woman still gesturing. I ignored her.

"Niña! Niña, me ayudas? Come help please!"

Seriously? What was that, Spanish?

I kept looking down the street, hoping Liam would show up so I would have an excuse to walk away from the crazy old woman.

"Me ayudas? You, niña! Girl, come help!"

She was only getting louder, and now someone had come out of the coffee shop and was looking at me funny. "Is she talking to you?" the woman asked, before tucking a strand of blonde hair back into her neat little bun.

Rolling my eyes, I got to my feet. "Unfortunately," I muttered.

I inhaled deeply on my cigarette before flicking it into the road ahead of me as I stepped down from the curb. Exhaling the smoke through my nose, I slowly walked toward the old woman. This was the last thing I wanted to do; the smug smile on her wrinkled face made me want to help her even less.

"Yeah? What?" I looked at her irritably, hands on my hips.

"Mi hijo, my son, he is very tired after working all day." The old woman looked at me expectantly.

So what? I really couldn't have cared less. Where was her son anyway? Was that the guy who went back in the hardware store?

"Well, that's great. Look, I'm meeting a friend-"

The woman grabbed hold of my arm as I turned away. She was pretty strong for an old, wrinkled lady.

"Help load into the trunk, sí? Por favor? Please?" She gestured toward the stuff stacked on the cart. "I could give you a..." she rummaged in the pocket of her colorful skirt, her tiny hand coming back out with a crumpled dollar bill. "A dollar, sí? For your trouble?"

Oh, yay, I thought sarcastically. A whole dollar – I could almost buy something with that.

Sighing, I reached for the first stack of wood and hefted it off the cart. "I'm good, thanks," I said, turning away from the hand holding out the dollar. If I moved fast I could get this done and escape the crazy lady before Liam showed up.

I heard a rattling noise behind me, and the bag of candy – red licorice – was shoved under my nose as I turned to get the next stack of wood.

"You like some, sí?" the old woman asked, pushing the bag toward me.

"Uh, no." I dropped the wood in the trunk and reached for some nails.

"Ah, so good, these." She was persistent, I'll give her that. "They sell them at check-out. It is why I come with my son." She cackled loudly, the bag of red candy shaking in her hand.

I suddenly felt a grin tug at the corner of my mouth. The old lady was kind of funny.

"So much better for you than that smoke, sí? That is no bueno, no good at your age, hmm?" She mimed holding a cigarette as I reached for another box of nails.

Okay, she wasn't funny anymore; now she had pissed me off.

Dropping the last box into the trunk, I slammed the lid down, causing the whole car to shudder and creak. "You're not my mom, and I didn't ask for your advice." I turned to stalk back across the street. Again, her hand gripped my arm, stronger than I expected.

"Sometimes the best advice is not asked for, sí?"

My eyes narrowed. "Not in my opinion."

I tried pulling my arm free, but the old woman held fast, her eyes looking at me in a way that made me uncomfortable.

"You are an old soul in a young body," she said finally, and released my arm.

I staggered back, staring at the crazy old bat before turning and hurrying across the street. An old soul in a young body? What was *that* supposed to mean? I shook my head, convinced the wrinkled old geezer had lost her mind.

"Hey, Vern!"

My teeth ground together as Liam yelled out from in front of the movie theater. I really hated when he called me that.

"What were you doing with the old lady?" Liam asked as I strode over to him.

"Helping her load her trunk," I said, not wanting to talk about it. I wanted to forget about the old woman and watch people get mutilated in the slasher movie. That would help me forget about things for a while; I needed to unwind and relax.

Liam threw his arm around my shoulders as we approached the ticket window. "You? Helping someone? That's funny," he said, barking a short laugh.

His words grated on already raw nerves. Why would it be so hard to believe that I would help someone? I shrugged my shoulders, dislodging his arm. "Whatever," I muttered, and stepped up to the window to buy tickets.

"We could sit in the back," Liam said, nuzzling the hair next to my ear suggestively.

"In your dreams," I snapped.

"Come on, Vern, don't be that way," Liam complained. He wiggled his eyebrows. "I made cookies this morning."

I stared hard at him. Liam never cooked, which meant they were marijuana cookies. I needed something to mellow me out, so maybe sitting in the back wouldn't be too bad...

"Come on," I said, grabbing our tickets and barreling through the door.

Wallace
18.

My pen tapped a random beat on the brochure from *Bernum School of Architecture*. I felt wired, but it was more from frustration than anything. The tension pulled the muscles in my shoulders tight, and my jaw clenched as I looked at the picture on the cover of the brochure. Questions whirled through my mind.

Why wouldn't Papá let our family be a part of my school project? What did he mean by saying it could be dangerous for our family? And why wouldn't Mamá and Papá agree to let me work my way through college? I wouldn't ask them to pay anything!

I avoided Papá and Mamá all day yesterday, trying to figure out an argument that would make them let me do the project about our family. And how I could talk them into letting me go to *Bernum*. I knew I would have to approach them with arguments they couldn't refute – and I would only have one shot. Papá was stubborn, and would shut down if I couldn't convince him the first time.

I also knew Emma would be wondering why I hadn't called for her and Veronica to come over to start interviews. It was Sunday, and the weekend was almost over. I would have to have a really good excuse in class tomorrow. Or a new idea for a project if I couldn't convince my parents.

Suddenly, I heard Abuela's voice through the thin walls, talking to Theresa in the kitchen. Maybe I could ask for her advice. I knew she wanted me to go to college. And if there were secrets in the family, she would know. Feeling more energized than I had all weekend, I jumped up from the bed, startling Mateo as he read a comic book on his bed.

"Not cool, bro!" he yelled after me as I bolted out of the room.

Thankfully, Theresa was leaving the kitchen as I entered. She ignored me, like she always did recently. Twelve-year-old girls were so…moody.

For a few seconds I watched Abuela knead bread dough with her small bare hands. Flour coated her fingers as they expertly manipulated the bread on the table.

"Idle hands are the beginning of evil, nieto," Abuela said without looking up.

My face flushing with heat, I moved over to the counter and grabbed the cooking pans. "Abuela," I said hesitantly as I set the pans on the table next to her. "Um, I wondered if you–"

"Both questions you seek answers for are best answered by your Papá, nieto," my grandmother said without looking up.

I stared at the silver hair pinned to the top of my grandmother's bent head. How did she know what I wanted to ask Papá? A second later, I realized what a stupid question that was. Abuela always seemed to know everything.

"He is in the backyard, nieto," she continued, still kneading the dough. The sleeves of her blouse were rolled up to her elbows, and I watched the tendons in her arms move under her wrinkled brown skin.

Sighing in resignation, I turned toward the screen door that led to the backyard. My grandmother's voice piped up behind me.

"Sé fuerte, nieto," Abuela said, looking up at me for the first time as I turned back toward her. "Stay strong."

She went back to kneading the dough, and I was left to wonder what in the world she meant as I went out the door to the backyard.

Papá had gone to the store yesterday, gathering supplies to fix a section of the short fence that wound around the yard. I could see him sorting boards and tools as I walked through the grass.

"Papá, could I talk to you for a minute?" I asked hesitantly.

Papá took off his baseball cap and wiped sweat off his forehead with the back of his forearm. He looked as resigned as I felt, and I began to wonder if he had had his own little conversation with Abuela. Papá rolled his hand in the air as he bent over the boards, his way of telling me to continue.

Thinking college would be the less explosive topic, I began there. "Papá, why can't I register for *Bernum School of Architecture?* I would not expect you to pay; I would work and pay my own way. But it is my dream to design buildings, Papá." My voice began to sound desperate, so I forced myself to stop talking.

Papá stood tall, his white t-shirt streaked with dirt and sweat. His hands were rough and calloused as he rubbed them together and took a deep breath. His eyes flicked past me to the house, and I turned to see what he might be looking at. I saw nothing and turned back toward him.

"Hijo, we know it is your dream," Papá began haltingly. He readjusted his cap, then seemed to make a decision in his mind. Abandoning the boards and tools, Papá gestured for me to sit in one of the plastic chairs situated on the small patio by the shed.

Sitting ramrod straight from the tension, my palms began to sweat and I rubbed them down the legs of my jeans. What was Papá going to tell me? He seemed so serious – and sad.

"Wallace," Papá began, leaning his elbows on his knees. "We would love to send you to that school. We know you would work hard, hijo. We have always been proud of how hard you work." He cleared his throat.

Then what's the problem? I wanted to yell.

Papá looked at me, then away toward the house. "Going to that universidad, there would be much paperwork required."

I frowned. "So?"

"Paperwork that would ask for proof that you are a citizen of this country."

I shrugged. "So we show them the visas, sí?" I was reverting to Spanish, which I only did when really nervous. I didn't understand what made Papá so upset.

Papá looked right into my eyes, and I was shocked by the sadness there. "There are no visas, hijo. Our familia is undocumented."

It suddenly felt as if all the oxygen had been sucked from my lungs. I sat, frozen to the chair, my hands clenching my knees so tightly they appeared to have no blood in them. A ringing sounded in my ears, and I felt the backyard recede as if I wasn't really sitting there.

"Wallace! Hijo, you need to breathe!"

Papá's voice cut through the fog surrounding my brain, and I sucked air in loudly. A few seconds ago my mind was frozen, paralyzed. Now it spun out of control. Fear was building, a terror I had never felt before.

"That...that means..." I still found it hard to breathe properly.

"We are here illegally," Papá confirmed, his voice suddenly calm. It was as if telling me the truth after all these years gave him a measure of peace. I wish I could say the same for myself.

"We could get sent back," I whispered, staring at Papá, though not really seeing him.

Papá nodded. "Theresa, Mateo, Lucas, and Gabriella were born here, so they would not be asked to leave. But, the rest of us..." he kept nodding. "Yes, we could be deported if anyone found out."

The pieces were falling into place in my mind. "So...that's why you don't want us doing the sociology project on our family."

Papá's expression turned grim. "Sí. If anyone finds out it is our familia – *your* family – it would be very bad."

I suddenly felt restless and sick to my stomach. I stood up abruptly. "I need to think."

Papá's voice stopped me only a few steps away.

"You must tell no one, hijo." His voice was hard. "*No one.*"

I nodded numbly, then almost ran for the house. The door slammed behind me, and I realized I was trembling as Abuela's eyes met mine over the dough on the table.

"Dejar la habitación! Out," Abuela commanded Lucas and Gabby. They were playing on the floor, and protested loudly as Abuela wiped her hands on her apron and shooed them into the living room area. Thankfully, Theresa and Mateo were in their rooms; Mamá was at work, having been offered double the money to clean a house today.

Abuela pulled out a chair and steered me toward it. I sank into it, still feeling numb. I put my elbows on the table, right in the middle of some flour, but I didn't care. I dropped my head into my hands.

"He told you, sí?" Abuela asked quietly so no one else would hear. She pulled a chair close to mine and sat down, leaning toward me.

I nodded, closing my eyes. "Why?" I whispered. "Why would you not come in legally?"

Abuela put her small, wrinkled hand on my arm, and I opened my eyes to look at her. "We did not have the time, or el dinero, nieto. What little we had was running out. Dinero, comida – money, food. Your papá's jobs kept getting cut short. One día, he received a letter from a friend about work in Texas. We decided as a familia that it was worth el riesgo, the risk, to come."

"I don't remember it being that bad," I argued, feeling anger mounting inside me, though I wasn't sure why.

Shaking her head, Abuela smiled sadly. "You would not, nieto. For your plate was always the first to receive food, and your clothes were the first to be bought."

I lowered my hands from my face and stared at where they lay among the flour on the table. "So I lose my dreams? I cannot go to college, to be an architect, because we are undocumented?" I couldn't bring myself to say illegal.

Abuela sighed. "Time will tell, nieto. However, you would not even have a chance if we were not aquí, not here."

Another thought fought for attention in my mind. "How do I tell Emma and Veronica why we can't do the project without telling them all this?"

My grandmother's face tightened. "I will speak to your Papá about letting you do the project."

Fear and relief collided inside. How could I be so afraid that our family would be exposed while still wanting to use our family for the project? And when did I decide it was okay to use our family anyway?

Abuela's hand patted my arm. "If you do not use names, no one will know it is our familia. They will simply think it is another from Méjico. But nieto." She leaned toward me, her dark eyes more intense than I had ever seen before. "The story of familias in Méjico needs to be told. Los Estados Unidos…they need to know."

I stared at my grandmother for a long time, then finally nodded. The words we had spoken days ago came back to me then.

Being different wasn't bad…it just didn't help sometimes. Maybe this was a way to make that better.

It took Abuela twenty minutes to convince Papá. Only twenty minutes. I couldn't believe it. When Abuela re-entered the house and gave me a firm nod, I went to my room and dug out my phone. Mateo was still reading his comic book and ignored me.

Sorry about this weekend – had to convince parents to let us interview them, I texted to the number Emma wrote on the paper in class.

I tapped the paper with her number against my leg while I waited for her to respond.

But we can?

Yes.

Let's wk out ?? tmrrw in class. FYI, V quit.

I stared at Emma's text, surprised. Then again, not so surprised.

She quit class this late in the yr?

No, school.

Fury swept through me, causing my jaw to clench so hard my teeth hurt. Veronica quit school? It took me a few seconds to work out why I was so upset, then it hit me. It was the injustice of the whole situation. I had to give up school and my dreams, and Ms. Attitude just gave up and quit for no reason? Why, because she was lazy? I had a thing or two to say about *that*. To her face.

My fingers flew over my phone as I shot a final text to Emma. Then I got up to find my shoes.

Emma

19.

I so did not want to do this.

Although it was better than being at home. Dad had stopped by to pick up more of his stuff, which resulted in a really awkward hug for both me and Hailee, and another yelling match between him and Mom. When I got Wallace's text, I grabbed my keys and tried to say good-bye over the screaming, though I doubt they heard me.

Turning the car onto the street my phone GPS told me to, I eyed the small houses and postage stamp yards. Some were run down and had garbage, broken appliances, and cars in the middle of their lawns. The house with Wallace's address may have had peeling paint, but it was clean and the lawn was mowed. A plastic tricycle was parked on the front walk.

Wallace jogged out the front door and hurdled the tricycle, making a beeline for my car. A little girl with black curls stood at the screen and waved, an apple slice in hand. She was cute.

"Thanks for picking me up," Wallace said as he climbed in the passenger side and shoved his glasses back up his nose. He reached for the seatbelt. "Mom has our car."

They only had one car?

Thankfully, I managed to keep my mouth shut and not spill out the insensitive question. "No problem," I said instead.

"So, how do you know where she lives?"

I pretended to be overly engrossed in backing out of his driveway so I could stall before answering. There was no *way* I was telling Wallace about my little beer binge. Finally, I mumbled, "You don't want to know."

Surprised when Wallace didn't comment further, I glanced over to find him staring out his window, the part of his face I could see appearing lost in thought. I wasn't sure what to say next. To be honest, the thought of seeing Veronica again didn't rate high on my list of wants in life. On the other hand, the other option was to go home to screaming parents. I already felt guilty for leaving Hailee there.

I just couldn't figure out why Wallace cared so much that Veronica was dropping out of school. We barely knew her, and she hadn't been nice to either of us at all. What did he care if she dropped out? I had been kind of relieved that I wouldn't have to see her again, even if it did mean more work on the sociology project.

We pulled into the trailer park where Veronica lived and wound through the streets. There were some run-down trailers and yards, and some well-kept, just like in Wallace's neighborhood. After a couple of short detours due to lack of street signs, we pulled up in front of Veronica's house. If Wallace was surprised by the broken steps and overall general neglect of the place, he didn't show it.

I had to hurry to keep up with Wallace as he got out of the car and leapt past the broken step onto the porch. It started to rain right then, and I wondered if it was some sort of bad omen.

Wallace didn't bother with the doorbell; his fist connected solidly with the door several times. I flipped up the hood of my sweatshirt, wishing I kept an umbrella in my car.

"What are you doing here?"

It was one of the first times I had seen Veronica without a scowl on her face; she was too surprised to frown, I guess.

"Can we come in? Thanks," Wallace said, pushing past Veronica and into the trailer.

It was a day for firsts. Neither Veronica nor I had ever seen Wallace so…aggressive. Or confident. Or mad.

"Get out!" Veronica yelled, whirling to face Wallace in the trailer.

I had stepped over the threshold with one foot, but slowly pulled it back onto the porch. Maybe it would be safer out in the rain…

Wallace ignored her comment. "You're not quitting school," he said, glaring at Veronica through rain-speckled glasses. His brown hair curled from the dampness of the rain, and with his new attitude, he looked like a completely different person. I had a hard time not staring at him.

"How-" Veronica stopped and turned very slowly in my direction.

I decided my decision of staying on the porch was a good one; if looks could kill, I would be six feet under right now.

"I didn't know it was a secret," I said weakly, lifting my shoulders in a small shrug. I felt my face get hot.

"I can do whatever the hell I want to," Veronica said heatedly. Her glare found Wallace as he stood with clenched fists in the living room. "Now get out of my house."

"Technically it's your parent's house. I mean, unless you pay for everything," Wallace amended. "No? Okay, well, are they here? Because I don't see them telling me to leave. So I'm staying."

Both Veronica and I stared at Wallace like he was an alien from another planet. What had gotten into him? Gone was the shy guy who hid behind his drawing notebook; I barely recognized him.

"What the-"

Wallace stepped closer to Veronica, cutting her off before she could finish. "Why are you quitting school?"

"That's none of your business," she growled.

"Why are you quitting school?"

Well, he was persistent, I'll give him that.

Veronica threw her hands up in the air. "No matter how well I do until the end of the year, I won't graduate. There – happy?"

"No."

The rain started to fall harder, and I inched through the doorway, praying Veronica wouldn't turn around and lambaste me for taking shelter.

"What do you want, Ace?" Veronica crossed her arms and glared at the boy in her living room.

"I want you to come back to school."

"Why do you care?"

"There are kids out there who never get the chance," Wallace spat, throwing his arm out to point toward the door and the rain now coming down in sheets. "Stop being selfish."

Veronica gaped at him. "Selfish? What good is it going to do me to go?"

"Any credit you finish this year will make getting your online diploma easier."

Man, I had to give Wallace credit – he wasn't even hesitating.

"I'm not going to get my diploma," Veronica shot back.

"What does your mom do for a living?" Wallace switched tactics without pausing.

Veronica was so caught off guard by his question that she answered right away. "She's a waitress at the bar down the road."

"And your dad?"

"Who knows?" Her eyes narrowed. "He's a bum anyway."

"So you're taking after him then."

My eyes widened in shock. Veronica took a step forward, her fist clenched like she was going to punch Wallace in the face.

"You're over the line, Ace."

"Not really. Just telling the truth."

"I swear, I'm-"

"Decide who you're going to be, Veronica," Wallace said, cutting her off without hesitating. "We'll see you in class tomorrow." He walked out the door and into the rain without a backward glance.

I hurried after Wallace, not daring to look at Veronica. The door slammed hard behind me. I ran toward the car, then stopped when I realized Wallace wasn't getting in.

"You got a tool kit in the trunk?" he yelled through the pounding rain.

"Yeah," I shouted back. Dad put one in there the day they bought the car for me. I had never used it.

"Pop it," Wallace ordered.

I opened my door and slid into the seat, reaching for the switch that would release the trunk. I saw it open from the rearview mirror, and Wallace bent down so I couldn't see him anymore. A few seconds later, he jogged back toward Veronica's trailer, red toolbox in hand. He couldn't seriously be going back in there?

Wallace stopped at the stairs leading to the porch and knelt down in the wet mud and grass. Opening the box, he took out a crowbar and hammer. I watched in amazement as he used the crowbar to pull up on the board that had fallen through the step, creating a hole. Once he had it repositioned, he nailed the board back into place.

Done, he tossed everything back in the toolbox and jogged back toward the car. I heard the thump of the box hitting the floor of the trunk, then Wallace opened the passenger door and slid in, rain dripping off him like he had just jumped in a pool. He took off his glasses to wipe them off, then realized he had nothing dry on his body to wipe them with.

"There is Kleenex in the glove compartment," I said, turning the key in the ignition.

"Thanks," he muttered.

The ride back to Wallace's house was quiet except for the windshield wipers beating repetitively as they swiped rain off the glass. We were still a few blocks away when Wallace said, "Sorry about the wet seat."

"It's okay," I said quietly, and meant it.

"We'll get started on questions tomorrow, and I'll find a night you guys can come over to start interviewing," Wallace said once we were parked in his driveway.

I noticed he said *you guys.* I couldn't believe how confident he was that Veronica would be in school tomorrow. I had my doubts. A lot of them. I nodded anyway.

As Wallace dashed through the rain to the front door, I pulled back onto the road, wondering if I had finally seen the real Wallace Perez. If so, I had a feeling I would really like his family.

Veronica

20.

I was so pissed I could barely see straight. How dare Ace barge in here and tell me what to do, how to live my life? And Priss! After everything I did for her this weekend, she repays it all by driving Ace to my door. I should have known better than to trust a rich snob. She just didn't get it.

All of a sudden I heard pounding, like someone was banging on something. I stomped to the window and yanked the curtain back – then stood there in shock as I watched Ace tear up and then nail down the broken board on the steps. My mouth fell open and I dropped the curtain.

Why would he do that? Especially after everything he just said. Who repairs someone's house after telling them off?

My body stood in one spot, but my mind was going a hundred miles an hour. I felt confused, pissed…just about every emotion I could think of. Suddenly the door flew open, and I whirled toward it, ready to give Ace a piece of my mind for coming back.

"You have no *idea-*" I began, then stopped abruptly as Mom looked at me in surprise. She shook out her umbrella and propped it against the wall.

"I have no idea about what?" she asked as she took off her soaked jacket and hung it on a hook. The hook looked like it was about to fall out of the wall, a piece of junk, just like everything else around here.

That pissed me off even more. "I thought – forget it," I said, waving at the air with my hand and turning away.

"Who was that driving away?" Mom asked as she untied her money apron from around her waist. "I saw a car pull out of the drive just as I turned the corner."

"Just some kids from school who think they know everything," I spat as I walked to a chair.

Mom looked at me, silent. Then, "Yeah. About school. I've been meaning to talk to you."

Great. I flopped down in the chair and leaned my head back, so not wanting to have this conversation right now. "I'm really not in the mood," I said, staring at the ceiling.

"Well, get in the mood," Mom snapped. "And start talking to me with a bit more respect."

My head jerked down and I stared at her in surprise. Mom sighed and sat down on the edge of a couch cushion.

"I got a call from school on Friday. You weren't there."

"Nope." I wasn't going to make this easy for her. I saw a muscle in her jaw twitch.

"The counselor also mentioned she had sent a letter home with you several weeks ago. One you were supposed to give me. About your status for graduation. It seems they had talked to you more than once about this." Her eyes narrowed and her head cocked to the side. "Know anything about that letter?"

I shifted my gaze away, refusing to say anything.

Mom sighed. "Veronica, why didn't you tell me before things got this bad? I could have helped with homework, I could have-"

Letting out a derisive laugh, I shook my head. "It wasn't because I couldn't *do* the homework, Mom. I didn't *want* to. So I…didn't."

She was silent for a moment, picking at a piece of dried food on her black pants. "Why?" Mom asked finally.

"Why what?"

"Why didn't you want to do it? Why don't you care if you graduate?"

I shrugged. "You didn't. Dad didn't. Thought I'd keep the family legacy going."

Mom's face flushed. "That was out of line, Veronica Jean."

That made me pause. Mom only pulled out my middle name when she was at the end of her rope.

"What does it matter?" I asked, toning down the attitude a bit.

"Don't you think we want better for you?"

"Dad obviously doesn't care; he's not here."

Mom's eyes slid closed for a brief second. "But I am. And I want better for you than waiting tables and bringing beer to men who have already had too much."

Something in Mom's voice made me look at her a little more closely. There was something in her eyes I hadn't seen before.

"It doesn't matter, Mom. I can't graduate this year, no matter what I do."

"So you're going to give up? Why don't you get your diploma?"

The tenuous hold I had on my temper snapped. "Why is everyone so concerned with me getting a stupid diploma?" I yelled, slapping my hands down on the arms of the chair.

Startled, Mom stared at me for a second. "Don't you want a career? When you were a little girl, didn't you ever dream of what you wanted to be?"

I shrugged. "Yeah, well. Reality check. Life isn't all princesses and ponies."

Mom suddenly looked sad. "Veronica," she said softly.

I stood up swiftly. "I don't want to hear it," I said shortly, and turned toward my room.

"What if I went back to school?"

Halting mid-stride, I looked over my shoulder in surprise. "What?"

Mom lifted her hands, then let them fall back in her lap. "What if you finish out the school year, then we work on getting our diplomas together?"

My eyes narrowed as I regarded my mother. She was serious. And nervous. Her fingers twisted together so hard it was like she was trying to break them. I didn't know what to say; I hadn't expected that from her.

"I'll think about it," I said finally, and went to my room, closing the door quietly.

Sinking down on the edge of my bed, I stared at a poster of the Rolling Stones. What few friends I had thought it was weird that I listened to such an old band, but I still thought they were great. Probably the one good thing my dad ever introduced me to.

I could hear Mom rummaging around in the kitchen. She was probably finding dinner and a beer; it's what she always did when she got home. Was she really serious about going back to school? Mom had never talked about doing that before, so why now? Just to get me to finish school?

Exhaustion swept over me, and I flopped backward on the bed. Staring at the ceiling, I wished it would all go away. I hadn't had this many problems before I met Priss and Ace.

My phone dinged, and I looked to see a text from Lindy come in; one from Liam was right behind Lindy's. I ignored them both and went straight for the music app on my phone.

Within seconds, "I Can't Get No Satisfaction" blared. I closed my eyes and let the music and words wash over me. Then "You Can't Always Get What You Want" came on, and I shut it off, irritated.

You can't always get what you want? I've *never* gotten what I want, I thought.

So why don't you start trying? a little voice in my head whispered.

I rolled over and stared at the poster again.

So why don't you start…

Wallace

21.

"You are beautiful, yes you are. Don't let anyone else tell you differently."

I rolled my eyes and grinned as I sat down next to Mason. He continued crooning to his tray full of food as if no one else was there.

"Hey," Damon said around a mouthful of sandwich. "You in for Imperial Wars again tonight?"

Shoving my glasses back up my nose, I shrugged before reaching for my own sandwich. "I'm not sure. I have that huge sociology project, and I'm not sure if my partners and I will be working on it tonight."

Damon's attention shifted to Mason. "Dude. Quit talking to your food and join the land of the living. Imperial Wars tonight? My place – you in?"

Mason squinted in Damon's direction, looking slightly offended for the food on his tray. "Yeah, sure," he said, then turned back to his tray and picked up his fork. I swear he started drooling.

"If I don't make it tonight, tell your mom thanks for the clothes, okay?" I said, looking at Damon over my bag of grapes. "We were able to use almost all of them, and it really helped my parents out."

Damon shrugged. "Sure."

A shriek had us – and most of the cafeteria – turning to look across the room. Sami Someone-or-other playfully smacked a guy at their table who was dangling a piece of wilting lettuce at her. I noticed Emma at the table, sitting really close to another guy. He leaned in close and said something that made her laugh. I stared for a second; I had never seen her really laugh, or even smile before.

"Rich kids," Mason mumbled through a wad of food. He shook his head. "They don't have the proper respect for food."

Damon and I looked at each other and smothered the laughs that welled up inside. "Yeah," Damon finally choked out. "No respect at all, man."

I took another bite of my sandwich to hide my smile. I purposefully didn't look around for Veronica. I wasn't stressing about it; she would either come or she wouldn't. It still made me angry to think of her quitting school while I had to give up *Bernum School of Architecture*, but I knew I couldn't let it get to me too much, so I tried not to think about it.

The bell rang, and I balled up my paper lunch bag and lofted it toward the trash sitting a few feet away. "See you guys. I'll let you know about tonight," I said as I grabbed my gear from under the table.

Maneuvering through the halls, I jogged down the stairs to the basement level and walked into Room 5. Emma and her group of friends weren't there yet, but they usually arrived right before the final bell. A quick scan of the room told me Veronica wasn't there either. Yet.

I took my seat and pulled out my notebook and pen. There was a note on the white board at the front of the room to start sitting with our project partners, so I made sure there were a couple of empty desks near me. Then I waited and started drawing a skyscraper.

Emma came in with her friends and glanced in my direction. She gave me a quick smile, which I wasn't expecting. The guy with the lettuce noticed and smirked in my direction, then turned and said something to Sami and the other girl…Tiffany? They both looked at me and laughed. I felt my face heat with embarrassment and watched as Emma's smile faded, but I noticed she didn't say anything. The guy who made Emma laugh at lunch gave her shoulder a squeeze before he turned to sit down.

Emma made her way over toward me, and I stood up to pull a desk close for her. "Thank you," she said softly. "Listen, I'm sorry about that." Emma glanced back toward her friends.

"Whatever," I said, brushing it off with a shrug. The last thing I wanted was to talk about it.

"Look at you, Ace. Finally found a pair of pants that actually fit, huh?"

I froze, my eyes locking on Emma's face as she stared in surprise over my shoulder. Turning slowly, I tried to ignore Veronica's rude comment and smile instead.

"Glad you could make it." I was half lying, and it came out through gritted teeth, but maybe she wouldn't notice.

Veronica smirked. "Yeah. Totally."

"We're glad you came, Veronica," Emma said, leaning out from behind me so she could make eye contact with her.

I pulled another desk close to Emma's, then retreated behind mine. Emma pulled out her own notebook and pen, immediately flipping it open to the notes she had started last week. Veronica slumped down in her chair and twirled a piece of dark hair while chewing a piece of gum loudly. Emma and I looked at her.

"What?" she snapped. Then Veronica noticed the papers in front of us. "Fine," she sighed, and dug into her backpack.

"So, on Friday you told me about some differences with your dad's work, Wallace," Emma began, and Veronica went on a deeper hunt in her bag for paper.

I doubted she would find any. I finally tore a page out of my notebook and slapped it on her desk, along with an extra pen.

"Thanks," Veronica mumbled.

My eyebrows rose slightly, not expecting that, but I kept my attention on Emma.

"Do you think he would talk more about that?" Emma asked me.

I shrugged nonchalantly, but felt tension seep into my shoulders. I was still nervous about what could happen to my family if this all went wrong. "Sure. My parents, uh, invited you both over for dinner tonight. And every other night this week if you guys want to come."

Emma looked surprised. "That is so nice of them!"

Veronica looked like she would rather do anything else than come over to my house, but she kept her mouth shut for once.

Again, I shrugged. "They know there is a lot to talk about, and if we want to interview everyone it will take some time. It would also give you guys a chance to see what differences there might be between how our family lives versus your families." I shuddered a little as I thought about what I was potentially opening myself and my family up to with Veronica and her attitude, but I didn't see any way around it.

Emma leaned forward slightly. "I can come tonight. What about you, Veronica?" She looked expectantly at the girl next to her.

Veronica sighed heavily. "Yeah. Sure, whatever."

Turning back to me, Emma asked, "What time should we be there?"

"Six-thirty. We eat a little later so Dad can get back from his job and eat with us."

Emma tilted her head. "You guys are a close family, aren't you?"

"Yeah, I guess so. We should figure out what we want to focus on tonight then," I continued, trying to steer the conversation toward something slightly less uncomfortable.

"Why don't we take tonight to just kind of get to know your family?" Emma suggested. "If the conversation happens to lead to something we could use in the project, that would be great. But I am really interested in just seeing how your family interacts and what some of the differences in how we live might be."

I nodded. "Sounds good." I turned to Veronica. "That okay with you?"

Veronica looked like we were asking her to jump into a pit of vipers. Swallowing hard, she finally nodded. "Yeah."

Emma glanced at the clock. "We have a few minutes left. Why don't we exchange phone numbers in case we need to get ahold of each other. Then we can go through and figure out what topics we want to hit on in the project and separate them into sections. After that, we can figure out how we want to get that information and how we want to present it."

The next several minutes were mainly a conversation between Emma and me, with Veronica grunting out agreements every once in awhile to make it appear like she was participating. Whatever. At least she was in school.

When the bell finally rang, Emma tossed her stuff in her bag and stood up. "See you guys tonight. Ian's walking me to class, so I gotta run," and she headed for the door where the guy from lunch waited for her.

Veronica shoved her still blank piece of paper in her bag and tossed the pen at me. "Thanks for the loan," she said as she got to her feet.

"Veronica."

She turned to look at me with a longsuffering expression. "Yeah?"

I stood up as well so I could look her in the eye. "You are welcome in my home. But if you dare embarrass my family in *any* way…you will regret it. Clear?"

Veronica blinked rapidly, her mouth slightly open in surprise. "Uh…"

I nodded. "Good."

Stepping past her in the aisle, I walked out of class without another word.

Emma

22.

"I'm glad you were okay last weekend," Ian said, tossing an arm over my shoulders. "I'm really sorry I didn't realize you were sick at the party."

I shrugged. "I kind of ran off without telling anyone; it wasn't your fault."

It was a short walk up the stairs to my next class, and Ian dropped his arm as we approached the door.

"I like hanging out with you, Em," he said, pausing a few steps from the door.

Blushing, I looked up at him. "I like hanging out with you too," I said.

Ian's face relaxed a little. "Maybe we can go out for a burger or something this week?" he asked hesitantly.

I looked at him in wonder. Ian was usually so confident about everything. "Sure," I said, smiling. My stomach jumped a little at the thought of going on an actual date with him.

"Great." Ian grinned. "I'll see you later, okay?"

Nodding, I turned to walk into class. It was then I remembered I might already have a "date" every night this week – with Wallace's family. "Shoot," I muttered. Now what was I going to do?

I didn't want to miss out on a date with Ian, but I really needed a good grade on the sociology project. I had a shot at being in the top ten of my class if I kept my grades up. Not to mention, my dad would kill me if I didn't do well on the project. If he even cared, I thought suddenly. It's not like he made much effort to talk to me or Hailee lately. Every time he did come over, it was to grab more of his stuff and get into another fight with Mom. Which was *so* fun.

Right at that moment, the loudspeaker crackled to life over my head.

"Emma Swann, report to the main office. Emma Swann, report to the main office."

Every eye in the class, including the teacher's, turned toward me. Well, that's not uncomfortable or anything. Mr. Randall waved me out, and I turned to escape the sea of stares.

On the way to the office, I tried to think why they would be calling me. Even knowing I hadn't done anything wrong, there was that slight feeling of shame I always got when called to the office. I turned the handle and walked in.

"Princess!"

"Dad?" What in the world? "What are you doing here?"

Dad feigned a hurt look. "Can't a dad stop by and drag his little girl out for some ice cream?"

Dumbfounded, all I could do was stare at him. Dad just kept smiling at me expectantly. Finally, I found my voice. "Uh, I still have two classes. There's still school."

Waving his hand in the air to dismiss my statements, Dad winked. "Life is short. Everyone should play hooky once in a while."

My jaw fell open. Who was this person? It certainly couldn't be my by-the-book-always-do-your-best father.

"Dad, what are you talking about?"

My father shrugged. "I just wanted to spend some time with you. You know, reconnect. Life is short," he repeated. He started to look a little irritated that I wasn't jumping at the chance to slurp up some sugary dairy.

Eyes narrowing, I stared up at my dad. I was getting a little annoyed myself. "Life is short, huh?"

"Yeah. Come on, Em, what's the big deal? Let's go get some ice cream."

"You moved out days ago. You didn't even talk to me and Hailee about it before you left." My voice was rising, and I could see the secretary's head peek around her computer. Dad started to look uncomfortable, but I didn't care.

"You just *left* us. Why, because life is *short*? What does that even mean, Dad? Did you get that from your little hooker?"

"Emma Ann, that was completely out of line!" Dad thundered.

Mrs. Lawson was on her feet now, looking concerned. Again, I found it hard to care.

"Is it? More out of line than screwing the woman who brings you coffee in your office and abandoning your family?"

"That's it! You're grounded!"

I glared at him with the most scathing look I could muster. "I don't live with you anymore," I said slowly. "You can't punish me. At. All."

"There are many ways I can punish you, Emma Ann Swann," Dad said, his face lined with fury.

Mrs. Lawson scurried around the edge of her desk. "Excuse me, is there something I can help with?" she asked breathlessly. The poor woman looked like she was about to have a stroke. This was probably more action than she had seen in all her years of working at the school.

"No thanks, I'm going back to class," I bit out, still staring at my dad. I turned to walk away, then stopped and turned back. "You know, Dad, we don't even realize you're gone."

Dad's face went red, then white in the span of a few seconds. "What?" His voice was much calmer now.

I shrugged. "You haven't been around a lot longer than the last few days. To be honest, we've been living without you for a long time." I looked hard into his shocked eyes. "Enjoy your ice cream."

I walked out of the office and into the hallway, my feet moving without my direction. It took a few seconds before I realized I was shaking. Badly. And I couldn't see. Tears were blurring my sight, and I stumbled on the tile floor.

I heaved a sob of relief when I saw the door to the bathroom, and I staggered inside, dropping my books and bag on the floor as soon as the door swung shut behind me. My body followed soon after, and I curled against the wall, my arms wrapped around my knees. Sobs wracked my body even as I tried to cut them off before they could escape.

What had happened to my family? We were torn apart, strangers. I felt like I didn't know who my parents were anymore. My chest ached as I thought back to when we used to order out for pizza and cuddle under blankets on the couch while watching a movie. We used to go on family bike rides and have picnics on Sundays at the park down the street. Sure, Dad was strict about school, but at least back then we knew he still loved us. He just wanted the best for us. What had happened to my family?

The door to the bathroom opened, hitting my books and scattering them across the tiles. I choked back a sob and scrubbed at my eyes with the sleeve of my shirt before daring to look up at the person who had caught me sniveling on the floor. My gaze locked with that of one Veronica Bennett. My heart sank.

Veronica let the door swing closed, then stood looking at me, hands on her hips. "I'm starting to see a pattern here," she said finally, head cocked to the side. "You know, with me finding you on the floor of bathrooms and all."

My face flamed and I scrambled to my feet. "I'm fine," I muttered as I bent to retrieve my books and bag.

Veronica smirked. "I can see that."

I chose to ignore her and slammed my books down on the counter instead, grabbing some paper towels and wetting them with cold water so I could wash my face. "What are you doing here, anyway?"

Veronica's eyebrows rose, and she glanced toward the stalls. "Well..."

I felt my face go red again. "Never mind."

"Relax, Priss. I'm actually here for something else."

My eyebrows rose this time, and I looked at her reflection in the mirror as she took out a pack of cigarettes and shook them at me.

"Want one?" she asked.

Was she serious? Of course she was. "No, thank you," I said stiffly, tossing the wet paper towels in the trash. Scooping up my things, I headed for the door.

"Maybe we can meet up again in Ace's bathroom," Veronica called after me. "You know, at dinner."

Thankfully, the door slammed shut before she could say anything else. Seriously, was I being punished for something? First my dad, then Veronica Bennett. Didn't I hear once that bad things came in threes?

I hurried to class and prayed it wasn't true.

Veronica

23.

I shoved the pack of cigarettes back in my bag as I watched the door close behind Priss. I don't know why I lied about coming in to smoke. Maybe it was the red eyes and red face from tears and embarrassment combined. Geez, I was getting soft. Why did I even care that Priss was crying anyway?

Because she reminds you of yourself, a little voice whispered in the back of my head.

Whatever, I snapped back, and dug in my bag for my eyeliner pen.

Darkening the lines around my eyes, I stared at myself in the mirror. What was I doing here anyway? I felt like an idiot for traipsing through school when I had no hope of graduating. It was stupid.

You can always leave and go home, the voice whispered.

Decide who you want to be, Ace's voice hissed back.

I slammed the top back on the eyeliner pencil. Whatever. I'd stick it out for today. I wasn't promising more than that.

* * * *

Squinting, I peered through the darkness at the small, brightly lit house. Seven-one-three Lighthouse Road. This was it. I pulled the car over to the curb.

I really didn't want to do this. My hands were slick with sweat, and my stomach rolled nervously. The reason why I was nervous eluded me. I only cared about this dinner so we could get the information for the project and get it over with.

As I got out of the car, I noticed a shiny white Lexus parked down the block a few yards away. That meant Priss was already here. Great. I had hoped we would arrive at the same time so I could shove her through the door first and keep the attention off me. Sighing, I headed up the walk to the front door.

The walls of the house were thin; I could hear children shrieking and laughing, and older voices talking through the door. The palms of my hands became even more damp. It sounded like the occupants of the house were having a great time. What was I thinking; what did they need me for?

I had turned to walk back down the porch steps when I heard the door open behind me. I tensed, my eyes sliding closed for a brief moment.

"Veronica?"

I turned to face Ace. "Hey. Thought I left something in my car, but I have it here." I patted the bag at my hip, the lie rolling easily off my tongue.

Ace grinned, and I stared at him in shock. He looked completely different. So...relaxed.

"Great. Come on in; my family is all here, and so is Emma."

Great, I mimicked in my head as I reluctantly followed him through the door. I pushed it closed behind me. It felt like I had just sealed myself into a prison. Granted, a brightly lit prison with a lot of happy people.

Priss sat on a couch that had seen better days, a girl with long dark hair sitting next to her, talking a mile a minute. Another little girl who looked to be about two years old was at Priss' feet, playing with a rag doll and leaning against Priss' legs as if they had known each other for years. Suddenly I wondered if she and Wallace were friends. Had she come over before? The thought bugged me for some reason, but I shrugged it off.

"I've got you now, haha!"

A menacing growl rose from the corner right behind me, and I felt a rush of air as a little body raced by me, then turned and shot a Nerf dart right at my chest from a plastic gun.

I felt the dart's impact more than I expected to, but it didn't hurt. The little boy, however, looked horrified, and dropped the Nerf gun on the floor as Wallace yelled, "Lucas! We don't shoot at guests!" The gun clattered across the floor and landed at my feet.

Bending down, I retrieved the complex plastic weapon and turned it over in my hand. I found the trigger. Looking at the little round face still staring at me in terror, I slowly lowered my bag to the floor.

"It looks like the tables have turned," I whispered ominously, and brought the gun up, pressing the trigger and sending a dart toward his leg.

The little boy named Lucas looked almost as shocked as his big brother. Almost. Ace was looking at me like he'd never seen me before. I ignored him; I had an enemy to destroy.

I sent a wink toward Lucas, and he grinned, then dove behind a chair just as I sent another dart in his direction. Hurdling a footstool, I twisted and sent several darts at once shooting in Lucas' direction. That little guy was fast; he was already gone and around behind another chair. All the darts missed Lucas by a mile, two of them hitting a man who was walking down a short hallway.

I immediately lowered the Nerf gun, my face flaming with embarrassment as the man looked down at his chest in surprise. When he glanced back at me, I had the vague feeling I had seen him before. His eyes lowered to the weapon in my hand.

"Ah, I see my youngest son has already corrupted our guest," he said, then smiled to let me know he wasn't mad. "And since my oldest is being rude, I will introduce myself." He stepped toward me and held out his hand. "Carlos Perez. Welcome to our home."

"Thank you," I said, releasing his hand as quickly as I could. "I'm Veronica."

We both glanced at Ace, who was still staring at me like I had grown another head. "Wallace, hijo! Have you introduced this young lady to your Mamá?"

Ace snapped out of his trance. "Uh, not yet. Veronica, why don't you follow me?"

I quickly handed the gun back to Lucas, giving him another wink, and walked by Priss on the couch. She smiled at me, but also seemed surprised that I had joined in the foam dart fight. Seriously, wasn't a girl allowed to have a little fun? In the back of my mind, I noticed that Priss' eyes still looked a little red.

Ace led me into a small, very warm kitchen. Two women were preparing food for dinner, both of them very short; I felt like a giant as Ace introduced me to his mother.

"Mamá, I'd like you to meet Veronica. Veronica, this is my Mamá, Isabella."

Isabella Perez hastily wiped her hand on her apron and grabbed mine with a surprisingly strong grip. "Bien – so good to meet you, Veronica." Her smile was wide and welcoming. "You are muy bonita, very beautiful." Isabella shot a sideways look at Ace.

I practically ripped my hand from hers. "Uh, thank you," I said, refusing to look in Ace's direction.

"My abuela – my grandmother – Ana," Ace said, also refusing to look anywhere near me. Instead he gestured vaguely in the direction of the woman at the stove.

The small gray-haired woman wore a brightly colored skirt that swished around her ankles as she turned to meet me. Her eyes locked with mine, and I felt my stomach drop to somewhere near the vicinity of my toes.

It was the old woman from the hardware store!

My face was hot from far more than the heat of the stove and oven, and I prayed Ace wouldn't notice. I had no idea what I should do. This woman probably hated my guts; at the very least she had to think I was a rude adolescent who should not be allowed into her home.

"Muy bonita, sí," the old woman named Ana said as she came forward to wrap me in a hug. Her eyes twinkled as she leaned back and looked into mine, and then I saw her wink. "Such a vibrant and healthy mujer joven, sí." Ana squeezed my arms and turned back toward the oven.

That was it? I thought for sure she was going to yell at me to get out. I looked at Ace dumbly, but he didn't seem to think anything was out of the ordinary.

"Dinner will be ready soon, hijo," Isabella said, looking at Ace. "Find Mateo por favor." She directed her gaze toward me. "Please, make yourself at home here in our casa."

"Thank you," I mumbled, and hurried after Ace.

"I'll be back in just a minute," Ace said, heading down the hallway his father had used earlier.

My fingers tapped my leg uncomfortably. What was I supposed to do now? Small talk wasn't exactly up my alley. Priss looked up and motioned with her hand for me to join her and the other girl, but my palms got sweaty just thinking about trying to have a conversation with those two.

"Miss V!"

I looked down in surprise to see Lucas standing at my side with *two* Nerf guns.

"Play?" he asked with a grin that was missing several teeth.

I grinned back. This I could do. "You're on!"

Wallace
24.

I could tell my parents were trying hard to appear as if they weren't uncomfortable.

No one but our family would notice the tension in Papá's broad shoulders. Emma and Veronica only saw his wide smile and laughter as he talked with them. They also wouldn't know that the long creases Mamá put in her napkin before unrolling it to crease it all over again was a nervous habit. Abuela didn't appear to have a care in the world, her aged face lined with laughter as she talked with Emma.

For myself...I was trying to hold fear at bay. Abuela was right – if we did not mention names in our report, or if we changed them, no one would know it was our family. No one would think to look further. *No one would know we were here illegally.*

I wish I didn't know. Life was so much easier when I didn't know. Between the knowledge of our lack of documentation, and the decimation of my dream of becoming an architect, the weight on my shoulders felt crushing. But I smiled and pretended that nothing was wrong, just like my parents. I thought I was doing a pretty good job. Until I caught Veronica looking at me across the table for the fifth time.

"The chicken burritos were delicious," Emma said, smiling at Abuela. "Thank you so much for having us for dinner."

"Such good manners," Abuela said, patting Emma's hand and beaming up at her. "Bueno, bueno."

Out of the corner of my eye, I could see Veronica sink a little lower in her chair. Gabby squealed in her high chair and reached out to touch Veronica's cheek with her sticky finger. Veronica winced, wiping at the spot on her cheek, but then smiled at my little sister. I had never seen Veronica smile before tonight, and it continually caught me off guard when I saw it; it was like a little jolt of electricity every time it happened.

"Let me help with the dishes," Emma said, beginning to rise from her seat.

"No, no. Wallace and Mateo will take care of that," Mamá said, taking the plate from Emma's hand and handing it to my brother, who groaned loudly. Let us go sit in the living room, sí?"

I glared a warning at my sulking brother as everyone got up from the table, elbows and legs getting tangled as we rose. We were usually cramped around the small space, but even more so with company. To their credit, Emma and Veronica hadn't seemed to mind.

Papá led the way, Theresa and Lucas following behind. Mamá reached for Gabby, then walked beside Emma to the couch. Where was-? I wasn't really surprised to see Veronica sneaking out the back screen door when she thought no one was looking. What did surprise me was the pack of cigarettes in her hand and the fact that Abuela followed her out the door.

I stood in the middle of the kitchen for a moment, completely mystified. Mateo's whining cut through my rambling thoughts.

"Come on, Wallace! I am not doing this by myself!"

Turning back toward the table, I grabbed a bunch of plates and silverware and deposited them on the counter. Mateo was already running water in the sink, so I hustled to get the glasses over to the counter, then started trying to find containers for the extra food.

It wasn't until I went to scrape out the crusted remnants of the enchilada pan at the garbage can near the door that the smell of cigarette smoke wafted across the night air and through the screen, overpowering the scent of Abuela's and Mamá's cooking. A low murmur of voices caught my attention, and I paused.

"...really okay by myself." Veronica's voice floated through the screen, sounding irritated.

"The Perez familia does not let visitors hide away by themselves without company," Abuela answered calmly, then gave a little sniff and cough.

I grinned. Dear Abuela, discreetly signaling that Veronica was being rude by smoking. I doubted Veronica cared enough to put out the cigarette.

"I've been on my own a lot," Veronica's voice replied without hesitation. "I can handle it."

"Mm. Life is so much more worth living when you allow people in, sí, mi niña?"

"Um, I'm not sure what you said at the end, but the first part hasn't exactly been my experience. And who said I don't let anyone in, anyway?" Veronica's tone had turned even more cross.

There was silence for several seconds.

"You have questions for mi nieto, my Wallace, sí?"

"Not sure what gave you that idea. Ace and I aren't exactly friends."

"You do not like my Wallace?"

My face burned as I stood frozen, the pan in one hand, spatula in the other. What would possess my grandmother to ask Veronica this stuff?

"Ace?" Veronica sounded as uncomfortable as I felt. "He's all right, I guess."

"Señorita Emma, you are friends with her, sí?"

"Uh, not really."

"Mm."

Silence. Mateo dropped a pan on the counter, making me jump guiltily in surprise. Still, I didn't move.

"I'm really okay by myself."

"It would appear not."

"Okay, *look* -"

"Wallace! Seriously, bro, I'm not doing this by myself!"

Mateo's loud complaint made me jump a second time, and I hastily scraped out the pan and moved back toward the sink. I kept an ear tuned toward the backyard, but couldn't hear any more over the running water and clanking utensils and plates. Disappointed, I picked up a towel and began drying the clean dishes.

It was only about a minute later that Veronica must have realized smoking wasn't worth the cost of having to listen to my abuela's opinions. She came stomping back into the kitchen, Abuela following behind serenely.

"Sorry, Ace, but I've gotta get going." Veronica didn't bother to look in my direction before making a beeline for the front door.

I glanced at Abuela in surprise. She looked back at me with a small smile curving her lips, then gave a slight jerk of her head as the door slammed closed behind Veronica. Sighing, I tossed the towel on the counter and headed after my classmate.

"Hey!" Mateo yelled indignantly. "No fair! I am not–"

It was suddenly quiet as I closed the front door after me and stepped into the cool evening air.

"Veronica."

"Forget it, Ace," she said, waving her hand in the air as she continued toward the road and her car. "It's not worth it."

Jogging to catch up, I touched her shoulder. "Hey, stop a minute."

Veronica stopped and swung around, looking like she was gearing up for a fight. "Why did you invite me here, Ace? So I could get a lecture from your family on how to live my life?"

I forced myself to remain calm. "No, I invited you here because we are working on a project together and need to talk to my family."

Veronica's eyes narrowed, and she stared hard at me. I kept my face as neutral as I could and looked back at her. Finally, her shoulders relaxed a little. "Your grandmother is nosy."

I shrugged. "Yeah, but she means well."

Agreeing with her threw Veronica off, and she smirked a little. "What about you, Ace? Do you mean well?"

Confused, I shoved my hands in my pockets. "What do you mean?"

"Why did you fix the board on my porch?"

"You would have tripped on it; it was dangerous to leave it like that."

Veronica cocked her head to the side. "Yeah, Ace," she said sarcastically. "Most people would have stopped to do that in the pouring rain after invading someone's house to yell at them."

I tilted my head back to look at the sky, frustration rising quickly. What was her problem? Granted, I hadn't tried very hard, but I could not figure this girl out. Finally, I lowered my head and looked her dead in the eye.

"I'm not most people."

"You're right," Veronica shot back, "you're weirder than most."

That was it; I'd had enough. "You know what? Forget it. Go home. I don't care anymore." I turned back toward my house.

"I never asked you to care," Veronica bit out harshly from behind me.

I swung back around, the part of me that couldn't stand injustice rearing hard inside. "No. You didn't," I said, taking a step toward her. "But that's what people do, Veronica. They care about each other, and try to help each other out. If you'd move out of your own way, you might actually see that."

"How dare you-"

"How dare I? How *dare* I?" I was full-fledged pissed now, and I really didn't care what I said. "How dare *you*? What did I ever do to deserve your nasty remarks and uppity looks? What did I ever do to you?"

Veronica stared at me with wide eyes as I stood in front of her, hands clenched into fists at my side. "You know," I continued, on a roll now and with no plans to stop soon, "you complain so much about Emma being prissy because she has money, but if you ask me, *you* treat people a lot worse than she ever thought to. So, yeah. Go home. My family doesn't need your poison."

I swung around and began stalking toward the house. Two steps in, I began to feel ashamed. I didn't remember ever talking to someone like that before, and while it felt good in the moment, it felt awful after. But I couldn't bring myself to turn around and apologize.

"Ace."

Veronica's voice was quiet; so quiet, I almost missed it. I didn't answer. I was ashamed of her, I was ashamed of myself, and I just wanted to go inside and be with my family. Yanking the front door open, I paused, then took my hand off the handle and left it hanging wide as I continued walking into my home. It was an invitation, and the closest thing to an apology Veronica would get from me. The question was –

Would she take it?

Emma

25.

I tapped my fingers on the steering wheel in time to the song on the radio. Before leaving the Perez house, we agreed that Veronica and I would come back right after dinner tomorrow night so we could talk more to Wallace's parents. At least, I planned to be there. Who knew if Veronica would show.

Talk about weird. She had stormed out of the house with Wallace running after her, and when he came back in, he looked madder than I had ever seen him. He left the front door open, but none of us saw Veronica behind him. About three minutes later, she came quietly through the door and sat down on the couch – and didn't say another word the rest of the night.

Shoving thoughts of Veronica out of my head, I thought of little Gabby instead. She was such a cutie. I had a lot of fun visiting with his family; they were really nice people.

As I turned the corner onto my street, I felt the car bump over something in the road. "Shoot," I said, glancing into the rearview mirror to see what I had run over. All I saw was a dark lump in the road, but my car was suddenly making a really weird noise up front near the passenger side. The steering felt a little funny too.

My heart hammering in my chest, I clutched the steering wheel and prayed I would make it to my house. I managed to pull into the driveway, but I could tell something was really wrong. Jumping out of the car, I rushed to the front passenger side, my phone on flashlight mode. I didn't need it though; it was obvious the front tire was completely flat.

Great. This was fantastic – just what I needed. Not. Sighing, I went back to the driver's side and leaned in to turn off the car. Grabbing my bag, I slammed the door and locked it, then realized how stupid that was since no one could steal it anyway with the flat tire. I probably should have taken my dad up on his offer to teach me how to change a tire, but it was a little late now.

I was still several steps from the side door when I heard the yelling. My heart picked up speed again, but I was confused. Dad's car wasn't in the driveway or the road, so who was fighting? My heart stopped. *Hailee.*

I ran the last steps to the door, my bag banging against my legs. Racing inside, I followed the raised voices until I came to the living room where Mom and Hailee stood facing each other, both mad, Hailee with tears on her cheeks.

"What's going on?" I asked, dropping my bag and walking to Hailee's side.

"Why don't you ask your sister?" Mom yelled drunkenly, stabbing her finger toward Hailee.

I stared at Mom for a second before looking at Hailee's terrified face. I didn't blame her; we had seen Mom wasted before, but this was worse than usual. And even though she had never hit us before, she looked mad enough to start swinging.

"What happened?" I asked Hailee in a low voice, keeping Mom in sight out of the corner of my eye.

"She says I threw away her wine on purpose, but I *didn't*," Hailee finished, leaning past me to glare at Mom.

I put my hand on her arm to keep her in place. My heart began to pound, fear moving through me. Mom paced back and forth with an odd look in her eyes, one I hadn't seen before. It made me wonder what she might do.

"Mom?" I asked, hoping she would clarify what had happened.

Our mother swung around, her face twisted in a furious scowl. "I woke up from a nap and went into the kitchen to get a glass of wine, but couldn't find any." Her words slurred, and I wondered how much she had had *before* her nap. "After searching the whole kitchen, I finally looked in the garbage can. Surprise, surprise," Mom singsonged, waving her hands in the air, "there they were – three bottles broken and heaped in the trash."

I glanced back at Hailee.

"I told you, I accidentally knocked them off the counter when I was getting the cookies from the cupboard," Hailee said, though there was less heat in her voice. "The bottles broke and I threw them away and cleaned up the wine. What's the big deal?"

"The big deal, *sweetie*, is that your oh-so-wonderful *Daddy* froze me out of our bank accounts today and I don't have any money to get more. You are always so clumsy," Mom sneered before lurching to the side and grabbing onto the nearest end table to keep herself upright.

My eyes narrowed. Ignoring the part about Dad, I felt myself bristle over the hateful comments toward Hailee. My sister's face was white, and I could tell she was trying not to start crying again.

"Mom, that was too far," I said angrily, wrapping my arm around Hailee's shoulders.

"I'm your mother, don't talk to me that way," Mom yelled.

"Then start acting like a mother and get sober," I shouted back, all thoughts of treading carefully flying out of my head. I couldn't believe she was acting this way.

"You hateful little witch," Mom shrieked, and picked up the book lying on the arm of the couch, cocking her arm back to throw.

"Hailee, go!" I shouted, using the arm around her shoulders to wheel her toward the mudroom. The book slammed into my shoulder as I raced after Hailee, and I felt tears fill my eyes at the pain.

Hailee's brown hair flew behind her as she ran full out for the mudroom door. I could hear Mom stumbling behind us, cursing as she ran into something during her pursuit.

"Emma, Hailee, wait! I'm sorry – I – " she swore as she collided with something that went crashing to the floor.

Wait? I didn't think so. My only thought was getting Hailee out of there. Too late, I remembered my bag and keys were in the living room. On the heels of that came the thought that I couldn't use my car anyway. I felt a moment of panic as we skidded into the mudroom, then saw Mom's keys on the hook near the door. Did I dare? Hell, yes.

"Go!" I yelled at Hailee, snatching the keys off the hook. "Mom's car! Go!"

We ran to the garage, and I felt a surge of relief as I noticed it was open. I hadn't thought to hit the button before leaving the mudroom. We scrambled into Mom's Nissan SUV and slammed the doors. My fingers shook as I tried to get the key in the ignition. I finally got it there, and the engine rumbled to life.

The SUV roared backward down the driveway as Mom flew out the door, her face tear-streaked as she screamed for us to stop. No way. At that moment, I didn't care how remorseful she felt; it was always too short-lived.

I got too close to my car and felt the jolt and heard the screech as I put a dent and line of scratches down the side, but again, I didn't care. We careened onto the street, and I heard a horn blare somewhere behind me as I slammed on the brakes and shifted into drive.

We traveled five blocks before either Hailee or I began breathing normally. My hands started to shake, and I clutched the steering wheel even harder. The SUV was silent. Finally, Hailee's voice, small and scared, came from the passenger seat.

"I did it."

"What?" I turned my head to glance at her, then returned my attention to the road.

"I did it. I broke the bottles on purpose." Hailee was sobbing now, and I felt my breath catch in my throat. "I knew she would be mad, but I just couldn't *take* it anymore!"

Her sobs were the only sound for several seconds, then I reached over and grabbed her hand. I didn't say anything; I didn't have to. My mind spun, trying to think of what to do next. Dad and our grandparents were out. They would try to take us from Mom in a heartbeat, and even as bad as things were right then, I wasn't sure I wanted that.

Ian.

His name flashed through my mind, but doubt came a split second later. Would he really want a girl he barely knew and her sister showing up at his door, begging for help? In the next second, I knew he wouldn't care.

"Hang on, Hailee, I'm going to take us someplace safe," I said, and spun the wheel to the left at the next corner.

Ian was as surprised to see me as I expected he would be. But he let us in. When his mom came to see who was at the door, I shook my head ever so slightly, and Ian made up some excuse about us being in the area and stopping by to say hi. Seconds later, we were in Ian's basement.

Hailee sank down on a couch and leaned her head back, obviously exhausted. I covered her with a blanket and told her to sleep for a while if she wanted. Then Ian and I went to the other side of the family room and sat on another couch.

"Em, what's going on? You're freaking me out," Ian said, leaning toward me a bit. He was looking at me like he thought I might break. When I looked down, I saw why.

My hands trembled so violently, I looked like I was having a seizure. Knowing Hailee was out of the house and safe was some kind of signal for my mind to let go, and suddenly my whole body was shaking. Tears welled up in my eyes, and I was horrified to feel them escape down my cheeks. I would become a blubbering mess in about two seconds.

"My mom – Hailee broke wine bottles – Mom threw a book – hit me – told Hailee to run." I hiccupped. "I didn't know where to go." The tears were coming faster now, and it was hard to catch a breath as the sobs wracked my body. Ian put his arm around me, pulling me closer, and I leaned my head on his shoulder, thankful that for one moment, I wasn't as alone as I felt.

When I finally calmed down, Ian and I talked quietly for a few minutes. There was no way I was taking Hailee back to our house that night. Asking Dad to take her was a non-starter – she wouldn't go anyway. Staying at Ian's would cause too many questions and would probably result in a phone call from his mom to my mom.

Finally, I snuck Hailee's phone out from under her limp hand and texted her best friend, Stacy. Pretending to be Hailee, I lied through my teeth about Grandma falling and being in the hospital, and Mom having to go see her, and could I stay overnight? I felt my shoulders relax more when I got a *yes*.

Then the question became – where would I go? Sami's house was out of the question; her mom and mine were too close. Tiffany annoyed me too much for me to handle staying at her house for longer than a couple hours. After several mental arguments with myself, and one vocal argument with Ian, I knew what I had to do – even though it was the last thing I wanted to do.

Packing a sleepy Hailee into the car with Ian's help, I dropped her off at Stacy's with the promise to pick her up from school the next day. Then I sat behind the wheel of my car, the dread mounting. I would have to drive over and hope she didn't kick me to the curb.

When had my life come to this?

Sighing, I put my foot on the accelerator and drove toward Veronica's house.

Veronica
26.

Well, this was unexpected.

I stared at Priss through the door. She wanted to stay *here*?

"What's going on, Priss?" I asked, not moving to open the door.

Priss looked as excited as I felt. "Look, I – I just need a place to crash for the night. I'll leave first thing in the morning, Scout's honor." She held up three fingers.

I cocked my head to the side. "Though I could believe you were a Scout, I'm not getting the feeling that's legit."

Priss' face flushed and she dropped her hand. "All right, fine. I know you'd like to think my life with all my money is great, just great, with no problems, but it's not, okay? My dad's screwing his secretary and moved out, and Mom's drinking more wine than I would have thought possible and came after my sister and me tonight. My sister is at a friend's house, and I need someplace to stay. Happy?"

She was looking at me with a red face, her chest heaving, and I suddenly had Ace's voice in my head. *"...that's what people do, Veronica. They care about each other, and try to help each other out. If you'd move out of your own way, you might actually see that."*

Priss' confession shocked me, which is probably what she wanted. To cover my surprise, I rolled my eyes and shoved the door open. "Fine. Mom's working late anyway."

I stepped farther into the house so Priss could come in. "Since you're well-acquainted with the couch already, why don't you take that?" I tossed my hand in that direction as if I didn't care, but something inside me didn't feel right. I wanted to get away from Priss as fast as I could. "Do you need a pillow?" I asked, begrudgingly, just wanting to go to my room.

Priss shook her head. "The throw pillows are fine," she said quietly.

I turned on my heel. "See you in the morning."

"Veronica?"

Halting, I waited without turning around.

"Thank you."

Hesitating, I nodded, then went to my room. Closing the door, I sat down on my bed and stared blankly at the wall. What was bothering me so much?

I know you'd like to think my life with all my money is great, just great, with no problems, but it's not, okay?

Priss' words rang in my head, and with them came a feeling of shame. I hated when people judged me because of my looks or my home. But Priss' words tonight showed that I had done the same thing to her.

"You need to decide who you want to be..."

Groaning, I pulled my pillow over my head and tried to drown out Ace's words. My life had been so much simpler before these people walked into it.

* * * *

When I walked out of my room the next morning, Priss was sitting on the couch with her knees pulled up, a small notebook balanced on top and the pen in her hand moving furiously. I hadn't seen either when she showed up on my doorstep, so they must have been in her jacket pocket.

Without saying anything, I headed for the cupboard and took out two bowls and a box of Raisin Bran Crunch. "Breakfast is served," I said as I grabbed two mismatched spoons from the drawer in front of me.

Priss looked up briefly. "Thanks." She continued scribbling in her little book.

I stood at the counter as I ate, the cereal crunching and breaking under the force of my chewing. My eyes narrowed as I watched Priss. "So what's next?" I asked abruptly.

Her pen halted for a second, then Priss finished whatever she was doing and folded the pen into the notebook, tucking both into the jacket lying next to her. "I'm going to eat." She got up from the couch and came over to the counter.

Rolling my eyes, I pushed my hair out of my face and squinted at her. "I meant about your mom, Priss."

She shrugged, trying to appear nonchalant. But I saw how badly her hand shook as she poured Raisin Bran into her bowl. "I'm going to talk to her."

"Hold on. *You* are going to skip school?"

Priss slammed the cereal box down on the counter. "Really? *That's* what you got out of that?"

I smirked so I didn't look like I cared too much. "Actually, I was wondering if that was a good idea." I paused, and Priss looked at me for a second before picking up her spoon. "I should go with you."

Priss dropped the spoon on the counter with a loud clatter, and I winced, knowing it could wake up Mom. She usually slept late into the morning after her long night shifts.

"Uh, no thanks, I'll be all right."

Relief swept through me, but I still wasn't sure she should go alone. "Are you going to Ace's tonight?"

Priss kept her eyes on her cereal. "Not sure. I'll see how things go with Mom. If I go, I may have to bring Hailee."

"Well, you have my number. In case you guys need a place to crash again." I raised an eyebrow in Priss' direction. "You know, just give a girl a heads-up next time." I put my bowl in the sink and grabbed my coat and bag from the hooks next to the door. "See ya."

I walked out the door, the irony not lost on me that I was heading to school while Miss Perfect sat in my kitchen, skipping for probably the first time in her life.

* * * *

Walking into the cafeteria, I scanned the room until I saw Ace hunched over his lunch. He sat with two other guys, a big chunky dude who looked like he was talking to his food, and a shorter, skinny guy with really bad hair. I headed in their direction.

"Hey, Ace." I plopped my tray down in front of him and slid into the seat, ignoring the surprised looks of all three guys. "Have you seen Priss today?"

Ace's eyes darkened. "I wish you would stop calling her that."

I lifted one shoulder in a shrug. "Yeah, whatever. Have you seen her?"

"No, why?"

Not bothering to answer, I scanned the room again. Liam sat at a table in the corner, looking at me with narrowed eyes. He jerked his head as if to tell me to come sit with him, but I shook my head slightly and moved my gaze along the side wall, looking for Priss. When I got to the table of rich kids, my eyes locked with that guy Ian that Priss hung out with. He was staring hard at me. It made me uncomfortable, and I moved on, finishing my scan of the room. No Priss.

"Hey, earth to Veronica."

Ace waved his hand in front of my face.

"What?" I snapped. Out of the corner of my eye I saw Ian get up from his table. Great.

"Why were you asking about Emma?"

I thought fast, not sure Priss would want me telling Ace what had happened. "Just wondered if she told you she might need to bring her sister Hailee tonight."

Ace's face relaxed. "Oh, that's fine. No problem."

Ian was walking toward us, and I didn't feel like getting into a conversation with Priss' worried boyfriend.

"Okay, great. See ya." I stood up, grabbing my tray as I walked quickly toward the doors. I dumped the food I no longer felt like eating in the trash, and tossed the tray in the bin on my way into the hall. I breathed a little easier, knowing Ian hadn't caught up with me. Then I felt the hand on my arm.

"Veronica? You're Veronica, right?"

With a longsuffering sigh, I turned and speared Ian with an irritated look. "Yeah. And?"

"Did she get to your house okay last night?"

I regarded the perfectly coiffed boy in front of me. He looked worried. "Yeah, she stayed the night."

Relief spread over his face. "Thank you."

I was suddenly afraid this would turn into some uncomfortable, sappy conversation, but Ian smiled and walked on down the hall. I stared after him. That was it? Okay, whatever. I hiked my backpack up, then checked my phone. I had no idea what Priss had decided to do about her Mom, but I figured I'd keep an eye on my phone in case she decided she wanted company for that conversation.

Heading to class, I kept my phone in my hand, then wondered when I began caring what Priss needed or wanted.

Wallace
27.

"You don't seriously believe her, do you?"

I watched Veronica disappear into the hallway, Ian hot on her heels, then looked at Damon. "Not really."

Mason shoved half a chocolate chip cookie into his mouth. "Why not? All she did was ask if Emma could bring her sister to your house." Cookie crumbs sprayed across the table, and I shook one off the back of my hand.

"Veronica wouldn't come over to talk to me about that," I said, staring thoughtfully at the door. "She wouldn't care enough to tell me that."

"Dude, maybe she likes you!"

Mason's eyes lit up, but Damon and I both shot him an exasperated look. "No way," we chorused in unison.

"So, you really can't come play Imperial Wars all week?" Damon was obviously done with the Veronica conversation. "Why do they have to come over to your house every night?" he complained.

"There's a lot that we have to research before we can really start putting it all together." I absently crumpled up my paper lunch bag. "I don't know, maybe it won't take as long as we think." My mind turned to Emma. Why had Veronica really asked if I had seen her today? Something didn't sit right about that.

"Hey, guys, I'll catch you later, okay?"

Damon grumbled something I missed, and Mason was too entranced by his last cookie to notice I left the table. Finding a quiet spot in the hall, I took out my phone and sent a quick text to Emma.

You ok?

My finger tapped on the side of the phone while I waited.

Yeah but won't be in Soc.

My brow wrinkled as I thought about that. She wouldn't be in class? Another text dinged in.

Hoping to make it 2nite.

I sent a thumbs up, but stayed where I was as the bell rang for next class. It wasn't like Emma to miss school, and why would she need to bring her sister tonight? On the tail end of that thought came the realization that it would just be me and Veronica working on the sociology project during class without Emma as a buffer.

Groaning, I shoved my phone in my pocket and headed to my locker.

* * * *

"Gee, Ace. You could look a little more excited to see me."

Veronica dropped her book bag next to her chair. I glanced up briefly, but really didn't want to maintain eye contact for too long so looked back down at the paper where I was making notes.

"Sorry," I muttered. "Just thought I'd make notes for tonight since Emma's not here."

Veronica didn't say anything. I read somewhere once that silence could be loud. I had no idea what that meant until just now. Even with the chatter of other students around us, the lack of conversation in our corner was deafening. My pen pressed harder into the paper, almost ripping the page.

"Look, Emma's going through something right now…"

I glanced up in surprise. One, that Veronica had said anything at all, and two, at what she said.

"What do you mean?" I *knew* there was something else going on.

Veronica fiddled with her notebook. She looked more uncomfortable than I had ever seen her. "It's not really my place to say, just – family stuff, okay?"

I kept my gaze on Veronica, not really caring that she was shifting uneasily in her seat. "How would you know that?"

"She stayed at my house last night."

Veronica flipped her hair over her shoulder with a defensive jerk of her head, and I felt my mouth drop open.

"She...stayed at *your* house."

Now really irritated, Veronica glared at me. "Yeah. She needed somewhere to crash."

I sat back in my chair, dumbfounded. "So she went to *you*."

Looking like she was about to come across the desk at me, Veronica's hand tightened on her pen. "Look, I don't get it either, but you said we're supposed to care, look out for each other, all that crap. So she stayed."

I had never been stunned speechless before, but I was now. There was literally not one thought in my head except for utter shock.

"Can we get started on what we need to talk about tonight?" Veronica snapped, flipping her hair over her shoulder again. "You're creeping me out with the whole staring thing right now."

"Uh, yeah." I forced my body to move, and straightened the paper in front of me. "Well, uh, I thought we could focus on some of the cultural differences tonight. But stuff other than just food, you know? Like views on jobs and families."

Veronica shrugged. "Sure. Whatever."

"Okay, well, um, Emma and I already talked a little about my dad's job and the differences in how projects are done in Mexico and in the U.S. We could keep going with that."

"I heard once that businesses are passed down to sons from their fathers for generations." Veronica's voice was hesitant. "You know, in other countries. That doesn't happen as much here. Maybe we should talk about that."

Forcing myself to look away from her, I scribbled that idea down at the bottom of the page, once again shocked speechless.

"*What?* For the love of – come on, Ace, you're acting like I'm an alien."

You are, I thought. *You're actually participating in the project, and we're having a normal conversation.*

"Just because I'm not graduating doesn't mean I'm stupid." Veronica's voice was steeped in venom.

And there we are – back to the Veronica we all knew.

"I didn't say you were," I responded quietly, hoping not to anger her further. "I really like your idea and think we should go over that tonight."

"Oh." Now she sounded a bit lost. "Okay, great."

I looked over at Veronica, deciding to take a chance.

"I don't have anything against you, Veronica. In fact, it takes a lot of guts to keep coming to school right now. And you have some really good ideas."

The look of stunned disbelief on her face made me feel awful. Her mouth fell open a little, but she didn't say anything. Then all of a sudden she jumped up from her chair.

"I've gotta go."

"What? Veronica, wait! Are you still coming tonight?"

My questions went unanswered as she disappeared out the classroom door, Ms. Hawthorne and half the class looking after her, the other half staring at me. My face flushed, and I sank lower in my seat and pretended to write something in my notebook.

What had just happened? I was just trying to be nice. It seemed like I could never do anything right where Veronica was concerned.

Emma

28.

There was no way I was going to text her to find out where she was.

After driving around for forever, trying to work up the nerve to confront Mom, I got home to find out she wasn't even there. My car was nowhere in sight, which meant she had the tire fixed and took off somewhere. I wandered through the house, wondering what in the world I was supposed to do now.

The book she threw at Hailee and me the night before lay on the floor where it had fallen. I picked it up, feeling the bruise on my shoulder as I did. Gently, I set the book on the end table next to the sofa.

My eyes moved to the mantel over the fireplace. A large family portrait hung over the fireplace, with several smaller pictures in frames lining the mantel. There we were, Mom, Dad, Hailee, and me. All smiling and in various poses.

I hated those pictures; they were a lie that never went away, on display for everyone to see. We looked so happy, but the truth was that we had all gotten into a screaming fight before leaving the house. I didn't even remember what it was about anymore. I do remember getting out of the car after a warning from Dad that we had better smile and act like nothing was wrong. So we started the lie with the photographer, then hung it for everyone who entered our house to see.

Unable to look at our smiling faces any longer, I turned away from the pictures and walked toward the kitchen. Right then, I hated my dad's job, I hated that Mom was a drunk, I hated everything about life. So I did the only thing I knew I had control over, at least for that moment.

I opened every cupboard, every drawer, searched every pantry shelf. Pulling out bottles of wine, vodka, rum, and beer, I shoved it all on the counter, pushing the bottles together so hard, I was surprised they didn't break. Then I moved to the master bedroom and bath. There had to be some there as well; I knew there were.

I descended the stairs with four more bottles in my arms. They joined the others on the counter. Pulling out a garbage bag, I took a second bag and opened it inside the first so the sides were stronger. Then I began dropping the bottles in, one by one. As they smashed together, I began to understand how much better it made Hailee feel to break those bottles of wine yesterday.

When the bag got too heavy and I was afraid the broken glass would cut through the bag and leak alcohol all over the floor, I opened another garbage bag. Then another. When the counter was clean, I carried each bag out to the trash bin by the house, hefted them inside, then rolled the bin down the driveway to the street. It wasn't garbage day, but I didn't want them anywhere near the house.

Then I went inside, sat at the kitchen table, placed my hands flat on the wood surface…and waited.

Mom walked through the door exactly thirty-three minutes later. When she saw me at the table, she stopped dead in her tracks. Her eyes met mine, and I felt my body fill with so much tension I felt like it would snap apart if someone touched me. I also felt more anger than I had ever felt before.

"Sit down," I instructed Mom quietly.

It was an out-of-body experience, acting like the parent to my own mother – and having her obey my command.

Mom sat down in the chair across from me, her handbag sliding from her fingers and down to the floor next to her chair. Her eyes were red, but I couldn't tell if it was from drinking or from crying.

"Where's Hailee?" Mom finally whispered, not taking her eyes off my face.

"Somewhere safe."

She flinched, and I was glad. I wanted it to hurt the way she had hurt us.

"I enrolled in an AA group this morning. The first meeting was at noon today."

Surprised, I just looked at her. That, I was not expecting.

Mom put her hands on the table, sliding them forward until they were mere inches from mine. They were trembling. I pulled mine back, but Mom kept hers there.

"I'm so sorry, Emma," Mom whispered, tears filling her eyes. "I can't believe I did that to you and Hailee; I won't ever be able to forgive myself for it."

"Good. You shouldn't." The lack of feeling I had toward my mother at that moment shocked even me. But when the one person who is supposed to protect you with her life is the one to attack you...something inside me died last night, and I wasn't sure if I could ever get it back.

Mom nodded, pulling her hands back and fumbling a napkin from the holder on the table to wipe her nose. "Will you come back? Where are you staying?"

I ignored her questions. "There are a few things that are going to happen."

Mom leaned back in her chair, but I could tell she was listening.

"You will attend those AA meetings every time the door opens. I don't care if that's three times a day. You go." I looked hard at her, shaking a little from daring to order her around, but knowing there was no other way.

Her eyes never left mine, and very slowly, Mom nodded.

"I have removed every drop of alcohol in this house, and if one can or bottle ever comes through that door again, I will call the police and turn in the pictures of the bruise on my shoulder from that book, and the written papers I have of everything that happened last night."

Wincing, Mom looked down at the napkin in her hands, the paper shredding under her twisting fingers.

"Hailee will only stay at the house alone with you if she is comfortable doing that. Otherwise, she comes with me, no matter where that is."

Mom put her elbows on the table and put her face in her shaking hands.

"And if you *ever* attack us again, I will take Hailee and we will leave, do you understand?" I leaned across the table as Mom gasped, her hands dropping from her face. "I turn eighteen in one month and I will take her from this house to live with me, and I will fight for custody with everything I have."

Mom's face was white as a ghost, but there was no sympathy inside me. When I left, I would break down, but not here. Not in front of her. I got to my feet.

"Emma-"

"No."

The hand she reached out to me shrank back into her lap.

"You did this, Mom. You and Dad. You did this to our family." Mom looked like I had slapped her across the face, but I wasn't through. "I will protect Hailee, no matter what it costs me, so don't try me."

I stared at the woman sitting at the table, but I felt like I had never seen her before. She was a shell of the person she used to be and was a stranger to me. I wondered if I would ever know her as a mother again. Time would tell.

I walked out of the house to go pick up Hailee from school.

Veronica

29.

I was surprised to see Priss' car pull up behind mine as I got out in front of Ace's house. Also relieved. It meant I didn't have to walk into the house alone.

"Everything okay?" I asked as Priss locked the door and headed toward me.

Priss shook her head. She looked completely exhausted, and there were dark circles under her eyes. "I have no idea. I talked to my mom this afternoon, and then got Hailee from school, and the three of us talked for a long time." Priss shrugged. "Hailee decided to stay at the house tonight, so that's something."

"She knows how to get ahold of you," I said encouragingly.

Priss looked at me with a surprised look on her face. Why was everyone always so shocked when I said or did something nice? It made me feel frustrated, and I looked away toward Ace's house.

"I'm not even sure I should go in there," I said, more to change the subject than to reveal any thoughts or feelings. "I think Ace's grandmother hates me."

"Why would you say that?"

I shrugged, not really wanting to get into the scene at the hardware store and the conversation from last night. "Just a feeling."

It was my turn to be surprised when I felt Emma's arm slide through mine. I stared at her tired face.

"Then we'll go in together and stick with each other during the night," Priss said, pulling me toward the house.

"You don't have to do that," I said, jogging a couple steps to get back to her side. It was a little embarrassing to think Priss thought she needed to hold my hand.

"Veronica." She stopped so suddenly, I almost pulled her over by walking another step ahead.

"What?"

Priss looked so serious, I actually stopped and waited.

"It's okay to have help sometimes."

Cocking my head to the side, I said bitingly, "Like you let *me* help today?"

Priss' jaw tightened, and I instantly felt bad. Why had I said that?

Instead of yelling at me, though, Priss suddenly sighed. "Yeah, well, maybe next time I'll take you up on that. It wasn't much fun doing that alone."

I looked at the girl next to me. "It wouldn't be much fun, no matter what. You're kind of tough, you know that, Miss Priss?"

She looked at me, obviously not sure how to take what I said. Then she threw her head back and laughed. "Not as tough as you, Veronica Bennett." Then Priss turned and dragged me up the front walk. "And now is your time to prove it." She reached around to knock on the door, then practically shoved me over the threshold when Ace opened the door.

* * * *

"Churro, mi niña?"

"Oh, thanks." I took the bowl of what looked like cinnamon and sugar dusted donut sticks and put one on the small plate in front of me.

They smelled awesome and I had to stop myself from taking a couple more.

"You can take dos, niña."

My face heating, I looked into the laughing eyes of Ace's grandmother. She gave me a saucy grin and plunked another churro on my plate before passing the bowl to Emma.

"Thanks," I muttered. Maybe Priss was right and Ace's grandmother didn't hate me too much.

The bowl made its way around the table, then found its way to the kids in the living room. Ace's parents had shooed them away a few minutes ago and told them to go play.

Carlos and Isabella smiled at us from across the table. "So where would you like to begin esta noche, tonight?" Wallace's father asked.

Both Priss and I looked at Ace, who rolled his eyes.

"Emma and I had talked before about how differently construction works here versus Mexico," Ace said, then paused to take a bite of his churro. I wondered if I should tell him he had sugar on his chin. Nah.

"And in class today, Veronica and I thought we should include the cultural differences between jobs and schooling in the project."

Ana clapped her hands beside me, making me jump. "Bien, bien! Excellent idea."

I blushed, even though no one was looking at me. I wasn't used to having people think my ideas were good. As I tried to discreetly fan my hot face, I realized I had blushed more in the last few weeks than I had in my entire life.

"So what more would you like to know?" Carlos asked, his gaze moving from face to face around the table.

There was an awkward silence, then Priss jumped in. "Wallace said that when someone wants to start a building project in Mexico, they just start building without really getting any idea of how much it would cost first. If the money runs out, they just stop."

Carlos and Isabella were nodding, but I looked over at Priss and Ace in surprise. Seriously? That sounded like a really stupid business plan to me.

"Is it like that with every business over in Mexico?" Priss continued. She had her pen poised and ready to write in the small notebook she always seemed to be carrying around. Too late, I realized I should have brought something to take notes with. I felt my face heat yet again. Great.

Ana nodded beside me, but it was Carlos who answered. He seemed to be a little more relaxed than yesterday, but maybe that was my imagination.

"It seems that in the Estados Unidos, the main care is dinero, money."

Priss' pen was going a mile a minute. How did she write that fast?

"Doctors, restaurants…they all want to get the next person in as fast as possible, only caring about how many they can take dinero from, not about taking orgullo, pride, in their work."

The churro paused halfway to my mouth. I hadn't thought of it that way before, but it was so true. How many times had the waitress brought the check early when I went out to eat with my mom? Though the times we had money to eat at restaurants were rare, it happened every time we did go out. And the doctors always seemed in such a hurry when I had to go in. I put the donut down and started paying more attention.

"So if everyone takes such pride in their work, do they in their schooling as well? Everyone is always bragging in the U.S. about what school they went to."

Wait, was that me? Priss looked at me in surprise, but Ace had a smile on his face. I looked back down at my churro.

"Buena," Ace's grandmother said next to me, patting my hand so hard I dropped the donut. "Buena pregunta."

I had no idea what a *pregunta* was, but it must have been good. Carlos was nodding again.

"There are many escuelas y universidads in Mexico. There is not so much a – how do you say it – pressure…to go to universidad as there is here. Many children go into the business run by familia. So there is not as much need for universidad.

"Must be nice," I muttered, then picked up my churro and shoved it into my mouth before Ana could make me drop it again.

"There is also the issue of money," Ace said quietly from the end of the table. I glanced at him, chewing quickly and double-checking to make sure I didn't have sugar on my chin. Ace still did.

"What do you mean?" Priss asked.

Ace spread his hands apart over his notebook. "There aren't as many people in Mexico with the money to attend college. But again, as Papá said, with all the tourism, the way to make money is through the family business. So college isn't needed as much."

"Orgullo," Ana said beside me. Everyone turned to look at her. "It is about pride. *Who* do you want to be? Your job," she waved her hand in the air dismissively, "it is not importante, sí? Who you are here," Ana tapped her chest, "is muy importante."

"So...be the person who does their job *well*, regardless of what job it is, or where it may lead. Like to success, or not," Priss said slowly.

Across the table, Carlos and Isabella beamed. "Sí."

I looked down at my sugar-coated fingertips. Ace's words from a few days ago rang in my head. *Decide who you are going to be...*

When I dared look up again, I glanced over at Ace's end of the table. He looked right back at me, then winked. I blinked, not sure I really saw him do that, but his attention was already somewhere else as he pointed to something Priss had written on her paper.

For what felt like the hundredth time that night, I felt my face turn red. I felt eyes on me, and looked beside me at Ana. For some reason she was smiling.

Wallace

30.

Mamá left the table to put Gabby to bed. Emma and Papá were talking quietly about his work with the local construction company. Thirsty, I got up to refill my water glass. As the water ran in the sink, I looked over my shoulder and saw Veronica move to sit in my chair. She put her chin in her hand and listened to Papá and Emma talk.

Water ran over my hand, and I looked back at the sink in surprise. I had let the water fill the glass and run over because I wasn't paying attention. Turning off the water and lifting the glass to my lips, I tried not to look back at Veronica. She seemed different somehow. Less...defensive, maybe? I wasn't sure, but she definitely seemed different.

Putting my glass on the counter, I turned around to see Veronica looking at the brochure for *Bernum School of Architecture*. She must have seen the corner of it poking out of my notebook and pulled it out. Suddenly, she squinted at the page below the brochure, at the doodling I had been doing. She looked from the drawings of buildings to the brochure, then back at my notebook.

Walking forward quickly, I snatched the brochure out of her hand and scooped my notebook up from the table. "It's rude to look through other people's things, Veronica," I snapped harshly.

The look of hurt on her face made me feel like the biggest jerk in the world. The surprise on Emma's face and the shock on my father's didn't help. I wasn't even sure what caused me to react like that toward Veronica. What did it matter if she knew I liked to design buildings?

In the next instant, the hurt in Veronica's eyes disappeared, and they turned hard, the impassiveness that always seemed to cloak her gaze falling back into place. The loss of the openness I had seen from her just a short moment ago felt like a sucker punch to my gut. I had no one to blame but myself for that.

"Look, I'm-"

"I should get going." Veronica pushed away from the table, interrupting my lame attempt at an apology.

"You don't have to-"

"I think we have enough to start working on the project," Emma said, cutting me off. She glanced at me and gave a slight shake of her head as if to tell me to leave it alone. "Maybe we can meet at lunch tomorrow and start putting it together? That way when we meet tomorrow night we know what direction to go next."

Veronica shrugged. "Whatever." She grabbed her coat and bag and headed for the door.

"Veronica, wait." For the second time in as many days, I chased her as she fled my house. I could hear Emma thanking my parents and Abuela behind me as the door swung wide and stayed there.

"Veronica, come on! I'm sorry, okay?" I tripped going down the steps and almost ran right into her as she stopped short on the walk and swung around to face me.

"What's your problem, Ace?"

Whoa. I took a step back, the fury in her eyes catching me off guard. I could understand her being angry, but wasn't expecting the rage that boiled in her gaze.

"Um..."

"Who do *you* want to be, huh, Ace?"

"Um..." I was at a serious loss. Why was she so mad?

"You're like two different people sometimes. Nice one minute, then pissy the next and yelling at everybody, telling them what to do."

My eyes narrowed. Really? "You're one to talk," I shot back, my own anger riding hard now. Forget the apology. "Who are *you*? Cause I've seen the pissed off bad girl and the semi-normal girl, but both keep disappearing, and it's getting kind of hard to keep track!"

"What the heck is going on with you two?" Emma ran up to us on the lawn, breathing hard from her run down the steps. She was still trying to get an arm into her jacket while juggling her bag and notebook.

"Apparently we're not allowed to know anything personal about Ace, here," Veronica snapped.

My eyes bugged out so far I thought they might fall out. "Are you kidding me? We're doing this stupid report on my *family*!"

"Wait, what-"

Emma's voice was lost as Veronica stepped forward, our toes almost touching.

"What are your dreams, Ace? Architecture school? You want to design buildings? Why is it a big deal if we know that?"

"It doesn't matter," I growled. "I'm not going to that school anyway."

"Wait, what-" Emma tried again.

"Why not? Money? They offer financial support. You can get help from the government."

It was like she slapped me in the face. I stood, staring into her face, her blue eyes lined with black, my chest heaving. The government. Yeah, the last thing they would want to do was help me. Deport me, maybe.

"It doesn't matter," I said again, hating the defeat I heard in my own voice. "I'm not going."

"You tell me to keep going to school, finish what I started, get the credits I can, and you're giving up on *this*? On your actual dream?" I had never seen Veronica so ticked off before. Her eyes flashed blue fire, and her cheeks were pink.

"What the hell is going on?" Emma yelled, throwing her notebook at both of us. Veronica and I were standing so close it hit us both in the arm, and we turned to stare at her in surprise.

Taking a step back from Veronica, I ran a hand through my hair, then pushed my glasses back up my nose. "Maybe my family is more important than my dream," I said, still breathing hard. "Not that it's any of your business."

"You know what, Ace?" Veronica stabbed a finger at me through the cool night air. "It's okay to be the kind of person who helps their family. But maybe living your dream is what would be best for them. Ever thought of that?" She took a step back as well, her eyes still flashing. "Why does *who* you want to be have to be separate from *what* you want to be?"

Veronica looked me up and down, and the disappointment I saw there cut me more than a knife ever could. "If you ask me, you're failing at both." She turned and stalked toward her car.

Emma and I stood on the lawn, staring after her. "Wow," Emma breathed, sounding afraid to speak louder than a whisper.

I ran my hand through my hair a second time. "Yeah. Wow."

Emma

31.

I tapped on my sister's door, then opened it. I had thought briefly about trying to talk to Mom, but her bedroom door was already closed, and I felt too exhausted from everything else that night to even attempt a conversation with her.

"Hey," I said quietly as I stuck my head around Hailee's door. "How were things tonight?"

Hailee pulled out her earbuds and gave me a small smile. "Pretty good. We actually played a card game for a while. I can't even remember the last time we played a game."

"Me either." I grinned, glad for my sister.

"Do you think she'll stay sober?" Hailee's face suddenly looked uncertain, and I opened the door farther and came in to sit on the edge of her bed.

"I don't know," I said honestly, wishing I could promise her something else. There was no way I would ever tell her about my conversation with Mom earlier that day, about taking Hailee with me if I felt I needed to. "But no matter what happens with Mom and Dad, we have each other, right? I'll always be here for you."

"Promise?"

My heart broke at how young Hailee sounded with that one word. "Promise." I reached over and ruffled her hair. "I'm going to bed. No worries, okay?"

Hailee nodded, but I knew she was lying when she said, "Okay."

I closed her door quietly and went to my own room. Flopping onto my bed, I lay back and stared at the ceiling. Even though I had run the conversation between Veronica and Wallace over and over in my head on the way home, I still couldn't figure out what had made Veronica so angry. I couldn't imagine it was just because Wallace hadn't told us about his architect dream. Was it the fact that Wallace wasn't going to college? If so, why did she care?

Suddenly, I sat up, feeling like a light bulb just went off in my head. Maybe Veronica wanted to graduate high school more than she let on. Maybe she wanted to go to college too. Could that really be it? Did she have a dream that she wasn't telling anyone? Or at least, not telling us?

I got up and started to pace, excitement building inside me. There were so many things I couldn't control right now. But maybe *this* was something I could help with. There had to be *something* Veronica could do to get enough credits to graduate this year.

My mind started flying in five different directions, the way it always did when I got a new idea for a story or writing project. I paced for another ten minutes, then grabbed my notebook, sat down, and began to write.

* * * *

"Over here!"

I caught sight of Wallace's waving arm through the throng of lunch students, and started making my way through the crowd.

"Hey, Emma, where are you going?"

Glancing to my right, I saw Sami waving me over from our usual table. She looked toward Wallace, then back at me, a look I couldn't read on her face. I could tell this was not going to go well toward my popularity. Then again, did I care that much?

"Hey, guys," I said, slightly breathless as I wove my way over to their table. "I've gotta work on the sociology project with Wallace and Veronica during lunch. But I'll catch up to you later, okay?"

Sami and Tiffany's perfectly plucked eyebrows rose. "Wallace and Veronica? What, are you friends with them now?"

I have no idea, I thought to myself. Out loud, I said, "We have to get started or we'll never finish it on time, that's all." Even as the words left my mouth, I felt slightly ashamed, though I wasn't sure why.

"Hi, Em."

I turned to see Ian walk up beside me. "Oh, uh, hi." Great. Was he going to give me a hard time too?

"Em is eating with her sociology buddies today," Sami said, smirking at me before turning back to her lunch.

"Oh." Ian looked surprised, then caught me looking over to where Wallace waited patiently, drawing in a notebook while eating a sandwich with his free hand. "Can I join you?"

"What?" My head snapped back toward him. That was *not* what I expected to hear.

"Can I eat with you? I feel like I haven't seen you in a while." He leaned close and whispered, "I miss you." Then he leaned back and smiled.

Oh my...I felt my stomach go haywire with butterflies as I looked into Ian's eyes. "Uh, yeah, you can eat with us."

"Thanks. Uh, shouldn't we go?"

"Oh, right!" I snapped out of my trance and turned to thread through the tables to where Wallace sat.

As I plunked my tray down and tossed my bag on the floor, Wallace looked up from his drawing. "Hey, Wallace. This is Ian."

Ian nodded as he set his own tray down. "Hey, man. What's up?"

"Um, hey." Wallace looked completely lost as to what he was supposed to say in response.

Ian didn't seem to notice, already plowing into the food stacked in front of him.

"Do you think Veronica will come?" I asked Wallace as I unwrapped the foil from around my turkey wrap.

"Yeah, I think she will."

The sound of Veronica's voice over my shoulder made me wince with embarrassment, but I tried to cover it up by turning to smile brightly at her. "Hey! How has your day been?" *How original, Em, what a great question.*

Thankfully, Veronica chose to ignore it and sat down instead. I noticed she left a seat between her and Wallace. Yikes. How was this going to go?

"So what is your project on?"

I could have kissed Ian for sticking his nose in and asking. Wallace gave him a short version of what we were doing, then turned toward Veronica and me. It seemed he was planning to ignore the huge yelling match he and Veronica had the night before. "Did you guys want to use the info we have as part of the interviews, or part of the main essay?"

The writer in me jumped to the fore. "I thought we could integrate the interviews as part of the essay. You know, make it more a narrative style? I would be more than happy to take the lead on writing it." I chose not to mention I had a bare outline and plan already written out in the back of my notebook.

"Sounds good to me. Veronica?" Wallace looked quickly at Veronica, then back at his sandwich.

"Yeah, whatever." She sounded bored.

I looked at her for a second, then decided to leave it alone. "Why don't you guys email me your thoughts and notes from last night then, and I'll start working on that. What do you want to talk about tonight?"

"What about individual interviews? Like, with my brothers and sisters?" Wallace shoved his used wrappers into his paper bag and crumpled it into a ball. Taking aim at the nearest trash, he sunk it without hitting the edges.

"Nice shot," Ian said, obviously impressed. I grinned.

"Thanks." Wallace gave a bashful smile.

"Sure. Look, I've got to run." Veronica stood up without looking at any of us, taking her uneaten food on her tray and dumping it all into the trash as she walked away.

"I would have eaten that," Ian whispered near my ear. I elbowed him in the side, hiding a grin.

Wallace looked after her, then quickly shut his notebook. "I'll go talk to her."

As he stood up, I hesitantly called his name. When he looked at me, I shrugged. "You chase after her a lot. Would it be better to leave her alone?"

Instead of being offended like I thought he might, Wallace looked toward the doors of the cafeteria, then back at me. "My abuela told me once that there are some people who need to be chased after."

He gave a two-fingered salute, then jogged through the tables, leaving me to wonder what in the world he meant.

Veronica
32.

I was not in the mood for this.

Swinging around to face Ace, I cut him off before he could speak. "You've got to stop following me around, Ace."

"No."

"What?"

"Not until you finally do something that makes sense to me."

I stared, not sure what he meant. "I don't get you," I finally sighed, turning to continue down the hall.

"Well, I don't get you either, but I'm trying." Ace fell into step beside me.

"Why?" I stopped again, wanting the answer more than I was willing to admit.

"Aren't you worth 'getting'?" he asked.

That stopped me cold. I opened my mouth to come back with one of my usual snarky comments, but nothing came out.

"I don't know." Of all the things to finally break through, *that* is what I said? I felt the start of a now familiar blush beginning.

Ace looked at me funny. "Veronica…" His voice trailed off.

"What?" I felt more uncomfortable than I imagined I could. What was it with this guy?

Suddenly, Ace grabbed my shoulders and pulled me forward, smashing his lips against mine. As kisses go, this was the most surprising one I'd had, that was for sure. Our lips were pressed together so hard I could feel his teeth behind his lips, and I hadn't had time to close my eyes, so I got an up close and personal inspection of his glasses.

Ace let me go as fast as he had grabbed me, and I pushed him, giving me an extra couple of feet. "What was that for?" I asked, completely shocked.

His face beet red, Ace stared at me, looking as surprised as I felt. "Um, not sure."

"*What?*"

Ace shoved his hands in his pockets. "I don't know, maybe it was…maybe it…"

I blinked rapidly, trying to piece together what in the name of all that was holy he was trying to say. "Spit it out, Ace."

"Maybe I was trying to show you that you're worth chasing after." The words came out in a rush, then I got a good look at Ace's back as he turned and raced down the hall away from me.

I felt frozen to the spot, staring after Ace long after he disappeared. At least there weren't many kids around. Most everyone was still at lunch or in class. Then I turned and saw Liam.

Why could I not catch a break today? It was obvious from Liam's expression that he saw the kiss.

"What the hell was that, Vern?" He came at me full bore, completely ticked.

The use of the name I hated got to me more than his anger. "What's it to you?" I shot back.

"Why is that geek touching you?" Liam looked down the hall, his hands curled into fists.

"Don't call him that!" I snapped, quickly working toward the same stage of fury Liam seemed to feel.

Liam turned to stare at me. "You saying that you actually *like* that kid?" he asked incredulously.

Now I was really pissed. "It's none of your business," I hissed, leaning closer to Liam to get my point across.

"Really? Cause I remember a few things going on in the back of a movie theater the other day that tell me it *is* my business."

My face flamed, but before I could respond, I heard footsteps coming up fast.

"Everything okay, Veronica?"

I turned to see Priss and Ian standing beside me, staring at Liam.

"Hey, the Richie-Rich kids are here," Liam sneered. "Get lost."

"Calm down, man, you don't need to be like that," Ian said, holding his hand out.

Liam knocked it to the side. "Get out of my face, Rich Boy. This doesn't concern you."

"That's where you're wrong," Priss said, dropping her bag and taking a step toward Liam. She had to tilt her head back to glare up into his face. "When you mess with Veronica, it does concern us."

Liam's eyes narrowed as he looked over Priss' head at me. It took me a minute to notice because I was staring in surprise at little Miss Priss. The girl had some guts.

"So this is who you're hanging out with now? Hell, Vern, I thought better of you."

"I don't think I'm that bad," Ian said, keeping his voice light. "Am I really that bad?" He turned toward Priss and me, his expression questioning.

"Can't blame a girl for stepping up in the world," I said, keeping my gaze locked solidly with Liam's.

His face red, Liam started toward me, almost running Priss down. Ian quickly moved forward and set Liam back with a hard shove to his chest. "Back up, man. It's time for you to go," Ian said quietly.

Sensing he wasn't going to win this one, Liam shot one more venomous look my way and stalked down the hall.

"Geez," Priss said, bending to pick up her bag. "What started all that?"

I opened my mouth, then realized if I told the truth I'd have to tell her about Ace's kiss. That was not happening.

"He's just a jerk," I said quickly. "He's always been that way."

From the looks Priss and Ian gave me, I could tell they knew there was more to the story, but they didn't press me.

"Well, are you okay?" Priss asked, her hand clutching the strap to her bag.

"Yeah, I'm fine," I said, wanting nothing more than to find a place to be alone.

"Okay. We'll see you tonight, then. Right?"

"Yeah. I'll be there."

Priss and Ian turned to walk away.

"Hey, Priss."

She turned back toward me.

"Thanks."

Priss shrugged, then smiled. "That's what friends do. They take care of each other."

Shaking my head, I watched them walk away, then made a beeline for the nearest bathroom. As I closed the stall door and leaned against it, I realized I was shaking. What surprised me even more was the knowledge that it had nothing to do with the confrontation with Liam.

It had everything to do with the kiss from Ace.

Wallace

33.

Idiot of the Year Award.

Guinness Book of World Records, here I come. What was I *thinking?*

At that moment, I was thinking that hiding in my room might be juvenile, but it worked for me. Emma and Veronica would be there any minute, and I had no idea what I was supposed to do or say to Veronica.

Why *had* I kissed her? Was I really interested in her that way? I had been asking myself that question for the last several hours and still didn't have a clear answer.

All I knew was – in that moment – she had looked so fiery and beautiful, her eyes sparking with anger and sadness, all at the same time. There had been a different side to her lately. I was really proud of Veronica for finishing the school year, even if she wouldn't graduate. As much as she infuriated me, I felt drawn to her.

The doorbell rang and I forced myself to open my bedroom door and walk into the living room. I pushed a smile onto my lips, hoping it didn't look as strained as it felt. From the odd look Emma gave me, I was guessing it didn't work.

Lucas suddenly flew past me, latching on to Veronica's waist. "Nerf wars?" he begged, tilting his head back to look in her eyes.

Veronica laughed, and I felt my stomach jump a little. Seriously, what was wrong with me?

"Sure, little man. Can I set my stuff down first?"

"I'll get the guns!" Lucas was off, almost mowing me down on his way to his room.

"You know, you don't have to do that if you don't want to," I said in a low voice. I didn't want her to feel obligated to run around the house after my little brother, dodging Styrofoam bullets.

Veronica looked at me with a gaze I couldn't read. "If I didn't want to, I wouldn't," she said flatly, then pushed past me to meet Lucas in the hall.

"Something going on I should know about?" Emma asked, her eyebrows rising.

My face instantly flamed hot, thinking about the kiss and trying to imagine confessing that to Emma.

Emma's eyes got wide. "Okay, I was just joking, but..."

Theresa saved me. "Emma! Come look at the poem I wrote last night!" My sister practically bounced into the room, her journal in hand.

After a last questioning look from Emma, I was left alone in the entryway.

"Nieto."

Almost alone.

I turned to see Abuela beside me. She looked far too satisfied to be up to any good. "Sí, Abuela?"

"Sometimes the mysteries of emotions are what teach us the most." She grinned.

"Huh?" I had no idea what she was talking about.

Abuela patted me on the arm. "You will see, nieto, you will see." She shuffled off to the kitchen.

Shaking my head, I walked into the living room and sat down, trying to stay apart from the rest of my family. Gabby was contentedly playing with her rag doll on the floor next to Emma, just like last time. Mateo was only in the room because Papá told him he had to be, and had his nose buried in a comic book. Papá was working late, and Mamá was in the kitchen making her homemade salsa for a snack later.

I wanted to stay out of the way tonight and let Emma and Veronica talk to my brothers and sisters. Though they wouldn't remember Mexico because they were born here in the States, they were raised in a home that honored our Mexican roots. They learned early that our family did things differently and ate different foods than their friends.

Veronica yelled out a truce, collapsing on the couch next to Emma and Theresa. Lucas groaned, then shot one last dart that caught her square in the stomach before giving a goofy grin. Veronica gave him a mock glare, then motioned for him to sit next to her.

"Do you ever read any poems or literary works by Mexican authors?"

I turned my attention to Emma's conversation with Theresa. My sister nodded enthusiastically. "I found several authors I like. I want to go to Mexico sometime to see what it's really like. The poems bring it alive for me, but since I haven't been there, how would I know if what they are describing is true?" Theresa shrugged.

"Do you like living here in the States, or do you think you would rather live in Mexico, where your family came from?"

I had never thought to ask my sister that, and I strained to hear her answer over Veronica and Lucas' conversation.

Theresa was quiet for several seconds. "I do like it here. But there are so many things I want to learn about where we came from. As much as Mamá, Papá, and Abuela try to teach us, there is only so much they can do, you know?"

Emma looked impressed with her answer. I was too; it was a very mature observation and thought process for someone her age. I really had no clue she thought that way.

"Sopapillas!"

I glanced over at Lucas, who had yelled out his favorite dessert. Veronica laughed again, and I had to work not to stare.

"What in the world is that?" she asked, shaking her head at my brother's enthusiasm.

Lucas shrugged. "Dessert. Mamá says they taste better in Mexico."

"They are deep-fried pastry dough pieces. Usually you put honey or cinnamon and sugar on them," I interrupted, wanting Veronica to have a clearer picture of what Lucas was talking about. "Different than churros," I added.

When Veronica's blue eyes met mine, however, I felt exposed for some reason, and quickly looked away.

"Salsa and chips de tortillas!" Mamá exclaimed, setting a huge bowl of tortilla chips and several small bowls of salsa on the coffee table. Abuela shuffled in holding a stack of paper cups and a pitcher of water.

My brothers and sisters rushed to the table, but Mamá clapped her hands sharply. "Guests first, mi niños!" They backed off reluctantly, but Emma and Veronica urged them forward again, joining them at the table this time.

I was scooping salsa with a chip when I heard Veronica's voice.

"What is the legal process for getting into the United States from Mexico? Is it really hard? I don't know anything about it."

Fumbling the chip, it landed in the middle of the salsa. Panic clawed at my chest as I scanned the room to find that Veronica had moved closer to where Mamá and Abuela stood at the edge of the room, patiently waiting for their turn at the table.

"I was wondering that too." Emma's voice rang out next to me as she walked past to stand next to Veronica. "The government always makes things so difficult, it must have been a lot of paperwork and red tape to get the right documents."

Mamá had a strained, panicked look on her face, and though Abuela stood expressionless beside her, I saw her wrinkled hand tighten where it lay on the back of a chair. I lunged forward, trying not to appear as freaked out as I felt.

"The process isn't really important," I said hastily, trying to fish my chip out of the salsa while seeming like I was just casually joining the conversation.

"It could be a good addition to the essay, even if we don't talk about it in the oral report," Emma said, oblivious to the panic she was causing in my family.

"No, I think we should stay focused on the cultural differences rather than how the immigration process works. That's a whole other topic."

"Well, I kind of agree with Priss on this one," Veronica chimed in, and I had to work not to throw my newly retrieved chip at her and yell at her to shut up. "It could add another layer of depth to it all."

I glanced at Mamá, who silently begged me with her eyes to do something. "I really don't think it's necessary," I said firmly. "We only have so much room in the reports and time to get this done. Adding more at this point wouldn't be a good idea."

There. That should work. I was pretty confident that I sounded casual about it all too. Then I caught Emma giving me that odd look again.

"Okay," she finally said slowly. "I guess we don't have to."

Veronica shrugged. "Whatever."

I felt my shoulders sag in relief.

"Nerf wars!" Lucas collided with Veronica's waist again, and she had to do some fast juggling to keep from dumping her food on the floor. I could have kissed my brother for his timing.

"Hold on, dude, I'm still eating!" Veronica laughed, reaching down to ruffle his hair.

"I'll find all the bullets and get the guns ready!" Lucas took off, and Emma scanned the room, her eyes landing on Mateo.

"I might talk to your other brother. Mateo, right?"

I nodded, feeling even more relieved when she walked across the room. Glancing at Mamá and Abuela, they seemed a lot calmer. Abuela gave me a small nod.

Even though I tried to enjoy the next couple of hours, I felt a level of tension that wouldn't go away. I could tell it was the same for Mamá and Abuela as well. I tried to mask my relief when Emma and Veronica said they needed to go, but I wasn't sure how successful I was.

Walking them to the door and outside, I stopped on the front walk, wanting to make sure they got to their cars okay in the dark.

"You go ahead, Priss. I need to talk to Ace for a minute."

Both Emma and I looked at Veronica in surprise, but Emma finally shrugged and gave a little wave. "Okay, see you in school."

I waited, but Veronica stayed quiet until Emma drove away. Then she turned to me, her blue eyes darker than usual. I suddenly felt like I needed to apologize.

"Look, Veronica, I'm sorry-"

"Ace-"

"No, I shouldn't have grabbed you like that. And kissing you without permission was inexcusable-"

"Ace-"

"I wouldn't blame you if you had punched me or something. I really am sorry, Ver-"

Suddenly, Veronica grabbed the front of my shirt and yanked me toward her. As her lips pressed against mine, it felt like the world shifted under my feet. My hands came up to her shoulders, but she let go as soon as I touched her and backed up a couple steps. I felt as if I had lost something when she moved away. Then she gave me a lopsided smile.

"Maybe I found out I like kissing geeks," she said quietly. Then she turned and walked to her car, leaving me in the front yard wondering if the kiss had really happened, or if I had imagined the whole thing.

Emma

34.

"It's so nice of you to want to help a friend, but the school has requirements that must be met, and there is nothing we can do at this point. You're support of Veronica is truly admirable..."

Blah, blah, blah. I stared at the tarnished bronze plaque telling me I was outside Room 5, but I couldn't bring myself to walk through the door. How was I supposed to face Veronica?

True, she had no idea I sent a letter to Ms. Anderson in the counseling office a couple of days ago. Yet. What if Ms. Anderson said something to her? Would she be mad that I tried to help? Either way, it didn't matter.

I had failed.

Why I even felt so strongly about the rejection of my letter, I wasn't sure. Maybe because I felt like Veronica needed this. She needed to have people back her up, she needed to know there were people she could count on. It didn't seem like she got that much at home.

The failure also meant I had come up short. Again.

I could hear my father's voice in my head, always telling me to do my best, to *be* the best. Yet, I couldn't manage getting to the top of my class, I couldn't get my writing published in any youth literary journals, I couldn't make it into the really popular group at school…I couldn't help Veronica graduate.

It was suddenly too much, and I turned around and walked back down the hall. Tears blinded me as I tried to navigate through the kids rushing to make class before the last bell. With everything going on with Mom and Dad, it felt like something inside me snapped when Ms. Anderson called me into her office.

I saw the doors in front of me, and I slammed against the push bar, breathing in the cool spring air as if I had been drowning. I hadn't even realized I felt so close to the breaking point until I wanted nothing more than to punch Ms. Anderson in the face for kicking Veronica to the curb. At least, it felt like she kicked Veronica to the curb. I did have to remember that Veronica's problems began with…well, Veronica.

But *still*.

I had never skipped school before, and now I was doing it twice in the same week. Life seemed so messed up.

I got to my car and drove out of the school parking lot, not even knowing where I was going. Driving aimlessly for several minutes, I finally parked at a lot that overlooked a large pond at the edge of town and just sat and stared out the windshield, my arms crossed.

It took me two hours to reach the conclusion that I needed to tell Veronica what I had done. She needed to hear it from me instead of from someone else, and she needed to know there was someone in her life who cared enough to try to help.

However, once I was parked in front of Veronica's house, I began to have second thoughts. Maybe this wasn't such a good idea. I put my foot on the brake to shift into reverse. That's when Veronica opened the door. Sighing, I put the car in park instead and got out.

"Priss? What are you doing here?"

I trudged up the steps to the door, the strap of my bag clenched in my fist. "I…kind of need to tell you something."

Looking confused, Veronica opened the door wider and let me walk past. My gaze landed on a Ziploc baggie of cookies open on the coffee table in the living room, and I felt my mouth water.

"Do you mind if I have one?" I asked, reaching in to take one before Veronica answered. Stress eating. It was a thing for me.

"Um, that's-"

"These are really good," I said, my eyes lighting up. I let my bag drop to the floor as I took a second bite. "Did you make these?"

"No, those are actually-"

I polished off the first cookie and reached for the baggie again. "Can I have another?"

Veronica's head was tilted to the side, and she was giving me an odd look. "What?" I asked around a huge bite of sugary goodness. Seriously, this was just what I needed.

After a second, Veronica shrugged, the corner of her mouth turning up a little. "Nothing. I'd stop at two though. They'll hit you harder than you think."

I squinted at her for a second, not sure what she meant, then decided I didn't care. I was already feeling better than I had all day; sugar does that to me. Flopping down into a chair, I finished off the second cookie.

"So. What's up, Priss?"

Was it bad that I didn't even mind her calling me that anymore?

"Okay, I don't want you to get mad."

Veronica looked at me strangely. "Why would I get mad? What did you do, Priss?" She suddenly looked wary.

I shifted in the chair, and rubbed my chest. The stress must be getting to me more than I thought; I felt kind of funny. Lightheaded, really.

"I wrote a letter to Ms. Anderson," I said meekly, not wanting to look at Veronica. "About you."

Her eyes bugged out. "From the counseling office? At school?"

I nodded, feeling an abrupt, irrational urge to giggle.

"Why would you do that?" Veronica demanded.

"I wanted to help you," I said defensively. It felt like I was about to jump out of my skin and I stood up, starting to pace. "I wrote a letter asking if there was anything we could do to help you graduate this year."

"That's none of your business." Veronica's voice had a hard edge, and I began wringing my hands. Why it mattered so much that she not get mad at me, I didn't know. We weren't exactly the best of friends.

"I know, I know." The words fell out of my mouth faster than usual. I really felt hyped up; I couldn't stand still. "Here." I jerked the letter out of my bag and shoved it at her. "You can read it. I really was just wanting to help," I repeated.

Veronica snatched the piece of paper out of my hand and unfolded it, her look incredulous as she stared down at my handwriting. I continued to pace as Veronica began reading, mumbling the words out loud every once in awhile.

"*Dear Ms. Anderson...am a friend of Veronica Bennett...was wondering if there was a program to help facilitate the expediency of bettering her grades so she could graduate...would personally take on the responsibility of tutoring Veronica...would be willing to be held accountable for her work progress...*"

Veronica looked up at me in disbelief. "You wrote this?"

"Um...yes?" I fought the urge to start giggling. It wasn't funny at all, but I couldn't seem to tamp down the impulse to laugh. A little hiccup of laughter escaped before I could stop it.

"Sorry," I gasped, holding my hands up as another giggle burst from my throat. "So sorry – I know this isn't funny-"

"Oh, come off it, Priss. You're high."

"What?" For some reason that made me laugh even harder.

Veronica jerked her head toward the baggie of cookies. "Those are pot cookies."

That sobered me up. "Pot cookies?" I asked blankly.

Veronica rolled her eyes. "Yes, Priss. Pot cookies. Cookies made with marijuana. You, Miss Priss, are *high*."

I stared at her, then at the cookies left on the table. A burst of hysterical laughter exited my mouth. "I'm really high?" I gasped through the giggling as I started pacing again. Tears began leaking out of my eyes.

"Oh, yeah. One would have done it, but you had two."

Stress eating just took on a whole new meaning. I was wringing my hands again, but oddly, I didn't feel upset. In fact, the whole thing seemed ludicrously funny.

"Sit down, Priss, you're making me dizzy with all that pacing."

I immediately sat on the edge of the couch, which made me feel like a puppy following orders. For some reason, I thought that was funny too and began laughing again. Not that I'd really stopped.

Veronica looked back down at the paper. I tried to stop laughing long enough to ask, "So, are you mad?"

Sighing, Veronica sat down in a chair and tossed the letter onto the coffee table. "No, Priss, I'm not mad." She paused. "It actually means a lot that you cared enough to try."

"Yes!" I flung my hand out, pointing a long finger at her. Which was warping and moving in an odd way. I squinted at my hand, then focused back on Veronica. "Yes, that's what it was! I was just trying to help; I wanted you to know we care."

Veronica was smirking at me, but I couldn't figure out why. My last sentence made her blink a couple times though. "We?" she asked.

I flopped backward onto the couch, my arms spread wide. "Me and Wallace, silly." I began giggling again. "We care what happens to you. Wow," I continued, rolling onto my side. "This stuff is crazy! I feel like my heart is about to run out of my chest."

"That's normal," Veronica said, but her voice was distant. So were her eyes as she stared somewhere over the couch.

"I've never done drugs before," I said, suddenly picking at a thread that seemed to change color right before my eyes. "This is weird."

Veronica finally focused on me. "I'm not sure I would classify it as a *drug*," she said, looking amused.

"You are a bad, bad influence, Veronica Bennett," I said, shaking my finger at her like my mom used to when I was little. Then I got distracted by the moving shapes on the ceiling and giggled.

"Do you really think Ace cares?"

I looked back at Veronica, who was looking down at her hands. She seemed uncertain, which was a new look on her; I had never seen that before.

"Of course! His family is so nice," I said, leaning my head back to watch the shapes on the ceiling again. "You want to know something funny?" I giggled.

"What?" Veronica was giving me that wary look again.

"For a second when we were talking to them about the process for getting the documents to come to the U.S., it was like they got really uncomfortable." I giggled again and waved my hand in the air. "But that's crazy, right? I mean," I let out a huge guffaw of laughter, "it's not like they're here illegally or anything."

I rolled back onto my side, clutching my stomach as I laughed, my heart galloping like a horse in my chest. Veronica was staring at me like I had grown another head, which I found even more hilarious and made me laugh even harder.

Veronica

35.

I felt frozen to my chair as Priss rolled around on the couch laughing like a hyena. The word illegal had paralyzed me. Why? Like Priss said, there's no way Ace and his family would be here illegally. Then why did I suddenly feel so uneasy?

My mind spun as I tried to backtrack and think if Ace had ever seemed uncomfortable talking about his family. I mean, we wouldn't be doing the project on them if they were afraid of being found out...right? It all sounded great in my head, but I still couldn't shake the feeling that something was wrong. And I hadn't been paying that much attention at the beginning of the project to know if Ace seemed uncomfortable or not.

"Oh, no." A set of new giggles followed.

Snapping out of my trance, I looked over just in time to see Priss roll off the edge of the couch, landing flat on her face. Seriously, this girl needed to stay away from alcohol and drugs of every kind. She obviously couldn't handle it.

Pushing out of the chair, I slid the coffee table over so I could reach Priss better and pull her back onto the couch. The only problem was, she was laughing so hard she was completely limp and no help whatsoever.

"Come on, Priss. We need to get you home."

And fast. Mom would be getting home any minute from the bar, and I didn't want her to know about the pot cookies. We finally seemed to have found some kind of shaky footing with each other. I laid off the beer and pot, and she actually signed up for classes toward earning her diploma. They started in May.

I found the cookies in my car this afternoon when I was trying to get a five-dollar bill that slid down between the console and the driver's seat. Liam must have dropped them when he leaned in to kiss me good-bye after the movie. I took them inside, planning to throw them away, but set the bag down and forgot. Then Miss Priss got greedy fingers and snatched two of them, and I somehow had to figure out how to get her home.

"Come on, I need you to help," I snapped, throwing my hands up in exasperation as Priss started staring at the ceiling again.

"Oooo, pretty," she said, her fingers moving as if she was touching whatever things she was imagining.

This wasn't going to work; I needed help.

Snatching my phone from my back pocket, I suddenly paused. Who would I call? Liam was definitely out. I actually hadn't heard from Lindy in awhile. Was she avoiding me? I should probably find out – later. Right now, I had to get Priss off my living room floor.

Ace.

I hesitated for just a second before hitting the call button. He sounded surprised to hear from me, but kind of happy, too. I felt a warm glow spread through my stomach as his voice came through the phone. Then Priss started giggling again, and I snapped back to reality.

After I explained what was going on, Ace promised to be there in a few minutes. He was as good as his word; ten minutes later he stood at my front door.

"Hey," he said, giving me a grin I hadn't seen before. It made my stomach go all funny again.

I couldn't help but smile back. "Hey."

"Oooo, is that Wallace? Wallace, come join the party!"

Rolling my eyes, I backed into the trailer so Ace could see Priss clapping her hands together like a little girl, still flat on her back on the floor. Her head was turned so she could see us as we came into the living room.

"Wallace, come see all the pretty lights! They're dancing!" Priss stared at the ceiling again, her eyes wide.

Ace's eyebrows met his hairline. "She seems...uh..."

"Stoned? Baked? Lit? High as a kite?" I cocked my head and regarded the girl I never thought would be blitzed out of her mind on my living room floor. "Yeah. That's our girl."

I heard a snort next to me and looked over in surprise to see Ace's face turn bright red as he tried not to laugh.

"From a *cookie*?" he asked, his voice unnaturally high.

"Well, two, if you want to be technical."

Ace ran a hand down his face, trying to compose himself. "All right. Okay."

I glanced sideways at him. "Giving yourself a pep talk?"

He glared at me. "No," he said shortly. "Trying to figure out how to get a girl who's stoned out of her mind in a car when she can barely walk."

Exhaling heavily, I put my hands on my hips. "Yeah, me too." We both turned to look at Priss.

It took twenty minutes, a broken picture frame, and an elbow to Ace's nose before we were able to wrestle Priss into the front passenger seat of her car. Ace's glasses were crooked as he backed out from fitting the seatbelt around Priss, who was suddenly seeing unicorns.

"Thanks," I said breathlessly as I reached to fit his glasses back onto his nose. It felt a little like we had just survived a war.

Ace's smile was as crooked as his glasses had been as he caught my hand in his before it could drop back to my side. "I'm glad you called," he said.

There was that freaking butterfly feeling in my stomach again. Flustered, I pulled my hand from his and shoved it into my pocket. "So, I'll drive her home while you follow, right?"

Ace nodded. "Then I'll give you a ride back here." He glanced through the window at Priss. She was using her hands to drum out a beat on the dashboard. "Good luck on the ride."

I made a face at him. "Thanks."

We climbed into the cars and headed out. Priss immediately punched the power button to the radio, then began switching stations every two seconds. It drove me crazy, but at least she wasn't having visions of unicorns prancing through a field or something. Then she started to sing.

Wincing, I slid as close to the driver's door as I could manage while still driving straight. As if that would help me get away from the screeching noise beside me. I really hoped Priss didn't have any big dreams of singing gigs in her future.

I literally sighed in relief when we pulled into Priss' driveway. Then I thought about her mom. Great. I hadn't thought this through; I didn't want to get Priss in trouble, and if her mom saw her like this…

Ace and I met up outside the cars, and I told him I would go see who was home first. Jogging to the door, I was relieved when it was answered by a girl a few years younger. "Are you Hailee?" I asked.

"Yeah," she said, a tone of suspicion in her voice. She kept glancing over my shoulder at Ace and her sister's car.

"I'm Veronica," I explained quickly. "Um, your sister came over for a little bit and isn't feeling so good. I drove her home, and Ace and I can help get her up to her room if you want."

Hailee's forehead creased. "Is she okay?"

"Oh, she's fine." *Stoned, and seeing visions, but she's fine.* "Is your mom home?"

"No, she went out for a meeting."

At least something was going in our favor.

Ace and I wrestled Priss from the car as Hailee stood in the doorway and watched us stumble up the steps and into the house.

"Hailee!" Priss said, her eyes moving spastically from her sister to other parts of the house, then back again. "I love you, Hailee," she sighed.

Priss' sister looked at me in confusion. "I thought you said she wasn't feeling well. Why is she acting so weird?"

"Oh, we gave her some meds at Veronica's house and it's making her a little loopy, that's all."

I glanced at Ace in surprise. I hadn't expected him to step up so quickly with an answer. He winked at me just as Priss slipped out of his grasp and almost fell down the stairs we were climbing.

"Easy does it, Priss," I grunted, holding her weight while Ace got her arm back around his shoulders.

After what felt like another war, Priss was tucked into bed with Hailee staring at her like she'd never seen her sister before. Ace and I saw ourselves out and climbed back into his car.

Once on the road, Ace and I looked at each other. He snorted again as he tried not to laugh, which made me chuckle, which made him start laughing. Pretty soon we both had tears running down our faces from laughing so hard.

"I mean, did you ever think you'd see Priss high?" I huffed out between giggles and hoots.

"She won't even remember this, will she?" Ace asked, flipping on the turn signal before making a left. He was still smiling.

I shook my head. "Probably not. We should have recorded it!"

Ace shot me a *look*. "Right. While we were manhandling her out of your house and into the car."

I shrugged. "It would have been hilarious."

Ace grinned. "Yeah."

A few minutes later, we pulled up in front of my trailer. "I'll walk you up," Ace said, unbuckling his seatbelt.

Surprised, it took me a minute to actually get out of the car. Liam always just dropped me in the driveway and then took off.

As we walked to the porch, Ace took my hand in his, giving me a shy smile. I smiled back, letting him hold it this time. As we climbed the steps, I eyed the board he had nailed back into place.

"I never thanked you for fixing the step," I said as we got to the door.

Ace shrugged, then tucked a stray piece of hair behind my ear. "I want you to know there are people you can count on, Veronica. You know that, right?"

I looked at him for a minute, my skin tingling where he still held my hand. "I'm beginning to."

And that scared me. I was beginning to count on Ace; I was getting used to having him around. Which made Priss' comment in the house that much scarier.

"Ace…" I hesitated. How do you ask someone something like this? "Your family…Priss said something…"

Ace looked at me with an expression I hadn't seen before. "What are you trying to say, Veronica?" There was an edge to his voice that hadn't been there before.

I squeezed his hand, not wanting him to pull away. But I needed to know; I had to ask. "You guys are here legally, right?" I asked in a rush. "I mean, you have the documents to prove that?"

For a second, I thought Ace was just going to turn around and leave, then he sighed. "Don't worry about us, Veronica. Please. I'm not planning on going anywhere."

He pulled me into a hug, and I felt relief sweep through me. Until I realized Ace hadn't really said yes. My hands tightened on his jacket, and I stepped closer. I felt his surprise, then his arms tightened around me. I closed my eyes, not wanting to let go just yet. There was a part of me that was afraid he would just disappear if I did.

After a minute, I opened my eyes – and looked directly into the gaze of Liam as he stood beside his car across the street. Ace felt me go rigid and pulled back, looking at me questioningly. Following my gaze, he turned to see Liam. Ace's features went dark.

"Shacking up with Tex-Mex now, Vern?" Liam looked even more pissed than he had at school.

"What are you doing here, Liam?" I said, keeping my arm around Ace. I felt a surge of panic, wondering how long Liam had been there and how much of our conversation he heard.

Liam ignored me, his eyes on Ace. "You should watch your back, Tex-Mex." He sneered. "She's got her own agenda, if you know what I mean." Liam circled around his car to the driver's side and roared off.

My arm dropped from around Ace.

"What's wrong, Veronica?" Ace asked. I noticed he still had his arm around me.

"Liam's right." I had to force the words out, because I didn't want to say them. "I'm not good for you, Ace. I don't know what I was thinking."

I tried to pull away, but Ace tightened his arm. "Look at me." I was so surprised by the authority I heard in his voice that I did. "I see *who* you are, Veronica Bennett. I don't plan on going anywhere."

Then his head bent, his lips pressed to mine, and I forgot about everything else. At least for that moment.

Wallace
36.

Why would Veronica ask me that?

Adrenaline caused by unease rushed through me, making it hard to focus on the good parts of seeing Veronica – like that last kiss.

Why would she ask if we were here legally?

I couldn't really ask Veronica if she heard something from someone, or why she asked without sounding guilty of exactly what she was asking about. Part of me wanted to talk to Papá about it, but what if it was nothing? Then I was worrying him for no reason.

I hated this. I hated the current of fear that constantly ran through me since Papá told me we were undocumented. How had my parents and Abuela lived like this for so many years? I didn't understand; there were so many things I didn't understand.

Pulling into the driveway, I hesitated before getting out of the car. I didn't want to go inside; I didn't want Mamá and Abuela to see panic in my eyes. Mamá had to run to the grocery store before dinner though, so I knew I needed to get inside to give her the keys to the car.

Sighing, I stepped out onto the driveway just as an older style blue Camaro roared up to the curb. My brow furrowed. Why did that car look so familiar? Then Liam got out, slamming the door behind him;

I noticed he left the car running. My whole body tensed as he came across the lawn at me.

"Hey, Tex-Mex. You need to stay away from Vern."

I looked at Liam's car, then back to him. He stood at least a head taller than me, and it was obvious he worked out often. Instead of being intimidated, I was ticked. Ticked that he would be so rude to Veronica, and treat her like property. She was so much more than that.

"Did you follow me here?" I asked, working to keep my voice calm.

Liam's eyes narrowed. "Doesn't matter." He reached out and jabbed a finger into my chest so hard it knocked me back a step. "Stay away from Vern."

"She can tell me if she doesn't want me around. She's a big girl." I reset my feet and felt my hands curl into fists at my side. If this ended up in a fist fight there was no way I would win, but I'd go down swinging.

The muscles in Liam's jaw tightened. "Who do you think you are?" he hissed, his voice rising.

I shrugged. "Well, my full name is Wallace Carlos Perez, but some people call me Ace."

I expected the first punch; my arm came up and blocked it just before Liam's fist reached my face. What I didn't expect was the follow-up from the other side. My head snapped back, pain exploding in my right eye and cheek. Suddenly I was staring at the sky and trying not to believe that I was going to die at Liam's hands, right there on my own front lawn.

Liam's shoes scraped through the grass, and I rolled instinctively, coming back up on my feet. I stumbled, my eye already swelling shut.

"You need to go back to where you came from, Tex-Mex," Liam growled.

His fist came at me again, but I didn't have time to do anything about it. I doubled over as it rammed into my stomach. Pain was everywhere, and I couldn't breathe. Liam pushed me over, and I couldn't stop him as he towered over me; my whole body felt paralyzed from the lack of oxygen.

Liam's hand grabbed the front of my shirt and lifted me a couple inches off the ground. He leaned over me, his breath stinking of cigarette smoke. "I'm not going to tell you again. Leave Vern alone."

A roaring engine and squealing tires ripped through the air, and Liam and I both looked over to see Papá's co-worker's truck skidding to a halt in the driveway, almost hitting our car. Papá was out first, but the other three men weren't far behind.

"Hey! *Déjalo en paz!* Leave him alone! *Sal de aquí!*" Papá was running at Liam, his face contorted in a way I had never seen before.

I found myself dropped unceremoniously back on the ground as Liam took off for his car. The door slammed and the Camaro roared down the road as Papá's hands helped me to my feet, his co-workers and friends surrounding me protectively.

"I'm okay, Papá. I'm okay," I gasped as air finally returned to my lungs.

"Who is he? Why did he do this to you?" Papá had reverted to full Spanish, and I tried to reassure him even though my face felt like it was on fire and I could barely see out of my right eye.

"No worries, Papá. Just a misunderstanding. It's okay."

Papá's friends offered to help me into the house, but Papá waved them off, thanking them for their help. He steered me toward the house, and I looked up to see a blurry image of Mamá and Abuela at the front door. They heard the commotion as Papá yelled and came to see what was going on.

Mamá looked horrified as she held the door open for us, and I tried to smile so she wouldn't worry so much. It only made her look more concerned, so I'm not sure what it really looked like. Abuela had disappeared and shuffled back to the chair Papá led me to, a bag of ice in her hands. She shoved it against my face, making me gasp from the sudden cold.

As I held the ice to my eye, I could hear muffled conversation between Mamá and Papá.

"...take him to hospital..." Mamá sounded frantic.

Papá's voice was a little calmer, but he seemed like he was agreeing with Mamá.

"I don't need to go to the hospital," I called from behind the ice covering half my face. "I'm fine, really."

Mamá looked doubtful as she turned to regard me, but Papá put a hand on her shoulder and spoke quietly. Finally, I saw her nod in agreement. I sighed in relief.

Abuela leaned toward me, a crooked grin on her wrinkled face. "Was it worth it?"

I looked up at her in surprise, then instantly regretted the fast movement. "What?"

"Is the girl worth it, nieto? Worth this?" She gestured toward the ice and the fact that my other arm was curled protectively around my stomach.

How did she know it was over a girl? Whatever, Abuela always seemed to know everything.

I stared off across the room, finally nodding. "Yeah. Yeah, she's worth it."

I didn't have to look up to know Abuela was smiling as she shuffled away into the kitchen.

Emma

37.

I was going to die. I was sure of that more than I had ever been about anything.

Trudging through the halls at school, my head pounded like someone was hammering nails into my skull. Ibuprofen hadn't touched the headache. At. All. Another kid's shoulder rammed into mine, causing me to jerk to the side, and my stomach rolled, the nausea I had been fighting all morning coming back with a vengeance.

I am never doing drugs or drinking ever again, I vowed as I headed toward the lunchroom. I wasn't even sure why I was bothering to go in there since the thought of food made my stomach heave.

The text from Veronica when I woke up that morning still rang in my head.

How those cookies treating u?

That began a long and heated texting conversation – albeit between stints of heaving over the porcelain throne – that revealed humiliating details I never wanted to hear again. Or have made known to the public. Ever.

"Whoa. What happened to you?"

I shot a venomous look in Ian's direction as he appeared beside me. He instantly threw his hands up in apology.

"I mean, you look as gorgeous as ever, Emma, and you look like you're having a...uh, great day."

I grunted, then tossed my bag onto a table and sat down, promptly putting my head down on folded arms. Ian took the seat next to me, the smell wafting off the food on his tray curdling the acid in my stomach.

"Seriously, Em, you okay?" Ian's voice sounded concerned, but I didn't plan on lifting my head anytime soon.

Lifting a hand to give an extremely sarcastic thumbs up, I wondered if someone really *could* die from a marijuana hangover. Because, seriously, I felt like the walking dead.

"Well, if it isn't Priss, all bright-eyed and bushy-tailed."

If I could have, I would have gotten up and punched Veronica in the face. I mean, I get that it wasn't her fault. Okay, whatever, I blamed her. Who leaves marijuana cookies out on their coffee table?? I lifted my head just enough to give her a pointed look that meant, *Don't tell Ian what happened.*

Veronica winked as she set her tray on the table. She was about to sit down when she looked over my shoulder and gasped. Anything that made Veronica react like that deserved my attention, so I slowly raised my head and looked over my shoulder. When I saw Wallace's bruised face and swollen eye, I jerked completely upright, forgetting about my hangover. Sort of.

"Who did that to you?"

I had never heard Veronica so angry, and seeing as how I had been on the receiving end of her wrath before, that was saying something.

Wallace didn't answer, just set his lunch bag down next to Veronica's tray and took a seat. Veronica didn't follow suit.

"Who did that to you, Ace? Was it Liam?"

My eyebrows rose. Why would Liam beat up Wallace?

"Sit down, Veronica," Wallace urged quietly. "I'm okay."

"Like hell you are," Veronica spat. She began scanning the lunchroom. "Is he in here?"

Wallace gently took Veronica's hand and tugged on it. She looked down at him, and they seemed to have a silent conversation. Veronica finally sat down, huffing out a breath in irritation. My eyes widened when I noticed that Wallace didn't let go of her hand. Instead, he laced his fingers through hers. What in the world had happened while I was drugged out of my mind? I looked at Ian in surprise, but he just shrugged and grinned before taking a bite of his sandwich.

I heard my phone vibrate in my bag, so I reached a hand in to dig it out. My head still pounded, but at least my stomach seemed to have settled down. Finally managing to extract my phone, I looked at it and felt my stomach clench all over again when I saw a text from Dad.

Can we talk tonight?

I only hesitated for a second before deleting the message without answering. I could feel Ian's eyes on me, but ignored him. I wasn't interested in hearing Dad's excuses about why he abandoned us. Mom was doing better; she should be at an AA meeting right about now, and Hailee said she and Mom had had a few good conversations now about it all. We were doing fine without Dad around.

"Do you guys want to come over after school today?" Wallace asked. "We could start piecing the project together in class this afternoon, then continue at my house. If we have questions, my mom and abuela should be around."

Even with the cacophony of noise in the cafeteria, our table had been so quiet that to hear Wallace speak gave me a start of surprise. It was a good idea, really. We only had another week to finish the project and give the presentation, so we really needed to get moving on it.

"Sounds good," I said, purposely ignoring my phone as it vibrated again next to me. Ian nudged me, but I shot him a glare and he backed off.

"I'll bring the cookies." Veronica smirked across the table at me. Even Wallace grinned, though I could tell his face hurt to do it.

Ian jerked in surprise, his eyes darting between the three of us. "Wha-"

My eyes narrowed. "You know, I never had to be carried home before I met you. You're a bad influence."

Veronica shrugged. "Yeah, I've been told that once or twice."

Rolling my eyes, I grabbed my bag and stood up. "I'm going to my locker."

"Wait up." Ian grabbed his bag of chips and sprinted after me. He caught me at the cafeteria doors. "Hey, what did that mean back there?"

"What did what mean?" I played dumb, hoping he would drop it.

"About being carried home."

"Oh, uh, well there was the party thing."

Ian ripped open his bag of chips and shoved three into his mouth. "I know about that one."

I sighed. "Okay, fine. I may have...tasted a few cookies at Veronica's house yesterday that had...a special ingredient in them." My headache was getting worse by the minute.

Ian's face screwed up in confusion. "I don't – oh..." Understanding dawned and he looked at me in shock. "You-?"

"I didn't do it on purpose," I snapped, refusing to look at him. "She didn't tell me they were...*those* type of cookies."

We walked in silence for a minute. Then I heard the unforgivable. A snort of laughter. I rounded on Ian, slugging him in the shoulder.

"It's not funny! I feel like I've got one foot in the grave," I complained, rubbing my forehead with my palm.

"Okay, okay, I'm sorry," Ian said, massaging his shoulder. "I, uh, think they have some meds in the office-"

"Hasn't helped," I interrupted, starting down the hall again.

Ian jogged a couple steps to get back beside me. "Well, you look kind of cute all hung over," he said, glancing at me out of the corner of his eye.

I stopped again. "You know, if you're going to lie, you should at least try something believable," I snapped.

Ian began backing away. "Maybe we should try talking later. You know, when the, uh, cookies have worn off." His eyes sparked with amusement.

"Yeah, like, a *lot* later," I yelled after him. Ian gave me a thumbs up over his head as he walked away, and I could tell he was laughing. I'd feel bad about yelling at him, but – he was *laughing.*

I turned and stalked in the other direction as my phone vibrated with a text for the third time. Rubbing my forehead again, I sighed. I had a really bad feeling about this day.

Veronica

38.

I pulled up in front of Ace's house, parking behind Priss' car. I felt ridiculous, being this excited to see Ace and his family. It wasn't exactly clear to me when they had become so important to me, but this...this was the best part of my day.

Hurrying up the walk, I reached for the doorbell just as Ace pulled the door open. "Saw you coming," he said with a grin.

To my surprise, he stepped out onto the first step, swinging the door closed almost all the way behind him. His black eye looked even darker in the shadows of the porch light, and I started to reach up to touch it, thinking how much it must still hurt. Ace caught my hand and pulled me closer, leaning his forehead against mine.

"I'm glad you're here," he whispered, and I felt a zing go through my stomach.

"Me too."

He brushed the briefest of kisses across my lips, but it did more for me than any other kiss I'd had before. The honest care I felt in that moment was so different from the demanding kisses I'd had from other boys.

Ace led me into the house, keeping my hand in his. I felt like everyone would turn to stare when they noticed, but no one seemed to think it was odd that Ace and I were holding hands. Emma grinned and waved when she saw me, and Ana came out of the kitchen and gave me a hug.

The hug stunned me, though I'm not sure why. I suddenly felt shy and unsure of what to say. Ana didn't say anything, however, she just released me, gave me a beaming smile, then went back into the kitchen.

Ace motioned to Emma, and she extracted herself from the adoring clutches of little Gabby. "We're going to use the kitchen table so we can spread our stuff out," Ace mentioned as he led us in that direction.

"Hola," Ace's mom said, smiling as we drew closer. Isabella carried water glasses to the table, then went back to the counter for bowls of tortilla chips and salsa. She set them down without a word and went back to the sink filled with dishes.

Pulling notebooks from our bags, we sat down and began comparing notes. "We should make an outline," I said, then felt uncertain. It's not like I had completed a lot of big projects for school – obviously. Maybe I should just keep my mouth shut.

"Great idea," Priss said, already flipping to a new page in her notebook. "I'll write, you guys brainstorm."

Twenty minutes later, we felt like we had a pretty good idea what direction we wanted to go with the project. Ace looked at Priss as she pulled a laptop from her bag and raised the top.

"Do you have PowerPoint with that?" he asked, and I could tell he had an idea.

"Yup. You read my mind," Priss said, looking up and grinning at him.

"It would make it look professional for the presentation," I chimed in. Then I realized I didn't know the first thing about using PowerPoint.

"Why don't I work on the oral presentation while you guys write the essay," Priss said, glancing up from her computer. "I know I said I would do that, but if it would be easier, I can just start preparing for the oral portion."

Ace nodded. "Yeah, sounds good. We can handle the essay, right?" He turned to look at me, squeezing my hand under the table.

Before I could respond, the doorbell rang. Isabella shook water from her hands and headed for the door.

"Okay, so this is what I was thinking…"

Priss' voice faded into the background as I heard something at the door that made my blood run cold.

"…been served."

My head snapped up, and I turned toward the door. Ace and Priss looked at me in surprise, but I ignored them, watching Isabella turn a white envelope over and over in her hands instead.

Sensing my unease, Ace followed my gaze and stood up. "Mamá? What is it?"

Isabella shrugged. "No sé, I don't know."

I couldn't say why, but my whole world felt like it was suddenly wrapped up in that envelope. My sight narrowed to tunnel vision, and I felt my hand grip the back of my chair as Isabella's fingers worked the flap on the envelope. Ace moved to stand beside his mother, looking over her shoulder as she scanned the paper.

Suddenly Ace's face paled, and the paper in Isabella's hands began to shake. "No. Hijo, this is a mistake, sí? How is this possible?"

Ace took the letter and the envelope, turning them over in his own hands, running his fingers over the seals. "No, Mamá." He took a deep breath. "They are real."

Ace turned to look at me, and I *knew*. Panic clawed at my chest as I realized I was about to lose everything I had just started to care about.

* * * *

I slammed on the brake, hearing the tires skid on the gravel as they locked to a stop in front of Liam's run-down house. The engine was running, the driver's door hanging wide open as I sprinted for the front door.

I didn't bother to knock; he didn't deserve it. Liam's mom dropped her cigarette in shock, and it bounced across the cheap card table they used as a dining room table. I ignored her, scanning the kitchen and dining room. Not seeing Liam, I stormed toward the living room.

"Veronica, dear, you should knock-"

I tuned out Liam's mom as I rounded the corner into the living room. Having heard my name, Liam was already on his feet, his video game paused on the screen of the flat screen television.

"Hey, Vern-"

My hands planted on his chest and I shoved as hard as I could. "You did this, didn't you?" I was yelling, but I didn't care. I watched in satisfaction as Liam tripped over the coffee table and almost fell. "You turned them in!"

Liam's face darkened as he turned to look at me after regaining his balance. "Yeah. Yeah, I did. Maybe that will teach Tex-Mex to keep his hands off you."

"It's not your place to decide who I'm friends with," I snapped. It felt like I was having an out of body experience, like I was separated from myself as I stared at Liam with hatred. I had never despised someone so much in my entire life. Not even my father.

"Look," Liam said, stepping closer, his face hard. "If they were legit, then nothing would have happened when I called. It's their own fault."

I couldn't even speak, I was so livid. *It was their own fault?* That was it? That was his defense? That was his excuse for ruining the best thing in my life?

"You know I'm right, Vern. That's why you're not saying anything."

My eyes slowly rose to meet his. "Oh, I have something to say. I just don't need words."

My fist lashed out and slammed into Liam's jaw.

Wallace

39.

"So it's true?"

Emma's voice was soft as she stood next to me on the porch, both of us staring down the road after Veronica's car. I had a hunch about where she was going, about what was happening in her head, and I should go after her, stop her. But I couldn't abandon my family.

Papá was on his way home, and Abuela had asked Theresa to keep all of the children in her bedroom while thwarting all questions Theresa threw at her. As she herded our brothers and sister into the small space, Theresa looked at me over her shoulder, and I saw the fear there; the same fear that was trying to paralyze me.

"Yes," I said finally. I didn't try to explain further. We had already talked enough about my family's life in Mexico for her to put it together. She was smart, she knew the truth.

Emma was quiet for several seconds. "What happens now?"

When my voice came, it sounded emotionless, dead. My mind felt sluggish as I tried to think through what was happening to my family right now.

"The paper said we have to appear before an immigration judge for a hearing. So they can decide if they are going to deport us."

"When?"

I shrugged. "It said it would probably be within a week."

"What can I do?" Emma asked quietly.

I looked down at this girl who I hadn't even known a few weeks ago and who I now considered a friend. But there wasn't anything she could do. I simply shook my head, not sure I could say much right then. "I'll keep you posted," was all I could manage, then I walked back into my house and the hell that waited there.

To my surprise, I found Mamá and Abuela at the kitchen table, my papers shoved to the side, other papers and forms in front of them. They looked much more composed than I felt. "What are you doing?"

They both looked up. Mamá finally pointed to the chair next to her, then turned a folder filled with papers toward me. "There are things we can do to fight this, hijo," she said quietly, so the other kids wouldn't hear. "We have researched this in case it ever happened to us."

"But *what* can we do?"

Abuela reached over and tapped a paper in the folder. "We have been in los Estados Unidos for over ten years. If we provide good character witnesses, proof that we are of good moral character, then they may cancel this."

"But they might not." I still couldn't put any emotion into my words.

Mamá shook her head. "They may not," she said quietly. "Hijo..." she hesitated.

I looked at her sharply. "What?"

Mamá looked at me with sadness in her eyes. "Hijo, you need to be prepared in case we have to..."

My gaze darted between Mamá and Abuela, waiting for her to finish, but knowing she wouldn't. From the looks on their faces, I knew what Mamá meant. I needed to be prepared in case we had to pick up and *disappear*. My stomach clenched. Anything but that, please.

"You *will* fight this, sí?" I'm not sure why the words came out. Of course they would. We had to stay here. My mind went to Mason, Damon, Emma, and Veronica. Of their friendship, and possibly more with Veronica. I thought of *Bernum School of Architecture*. If we left, I would have no hope of finding a way to attend. My dream would be over.

Mamá and Abuela had been silent too long. My gaze darted between them. "We *will* fight." It sounded like an order, and I meant it as one. We couldn't leave.

"Abuela and I will speak to Papá when he gets home," Mamá said softly. Her tone told me that arguing right then would not be a good thing.

I felt numb as I rose from the table and went to my room. Lying down on my bed, I stared at the ceiling above me. Why had this happened? I was mad, I was terrified, I was a thousand emotions I couldn't define.

My elbow slid across something on the bed and I looked down to see my drawing notebook. Sitting up, I pulled it out from under me and flipped through the pages, looking at the designs, the buildings I had hoped to build some day.

Then I slammed the cover shut and threw the book across the room, watching as it hit the wall and slid to the floor.

Emma

40.

I had driven to Walton City Park and had been pacing for twenty minutes. Jittery and filled with dread, I felt like I was going to be sick as I thought about Wallace and his family. They were going to be deported, I knew it.

While I didn't know a lot about the politics of the world, I did know that the U.S. government had recently put new laws into effect regarding illegal immigrants. It had been on television on a night when I was bored and surfing channels. Even if they chose to fight the deportation, they wouldn't win.

The brochure for the college Wallace wanted to attend flashed through my mind. What was it? *Burton Architecture? Bailey's Architecture School?* Frustrated that I couldn't remember, I picked up a stick and threw it in the creek beside me. Either way, it didn't matter. He had no hope of going to that school now. He had no hope of ever achieving his dream.

The injustice of it all had tears leaking out of the corners of my eyes. Sure, maybe they should have come to the country legally, but things happened, right? They were trying to keep their family together, trying to keep everyone safe, trying to give their kids the opportunities they never had. Now they were being punished for it.

How hard was it to get a visa for the U.S. anyway? I stopped pacing, my body suddenly going very still. Wasn't there something like a student visa?

Yanking my phone from my pocket, I punched Ian's number. He loved law and was hoping to get into Harvard if his grades were good enough. He would know this.

When Ian answered, I talked so fast he had to make me repeat everything. I fought not to snap at him even though I felt like time was running out, that we had to do something *now*.

I began pacing again as I listened to Ian, my mind running at a hundred miles per hour. When I got off the phone with him, I flipped to the web browser on my phone and began looking up the college I had finally remembered the name for. In five minutes I was back in my car and headed to talk to the one person I really didn't want to, but who was the only one who could help me.

* * * *

The door swung open wide, and Dad stared at me. I ignored him, glancing past him into his apartment looking for *her*. The last thing I needed was to run into his girlfriend on top of everything else. I wouldn't be held responsible for my actions if that happened.

"She's not here," Dad said, a note of weariness in his voice.

"Good." I shoved past him and into the apartment.

"Ever thought about answering the texts I sent you earlier today?" Dad asked as he swung the door closed again.

"I didn't want to." I knew I was being a brat, but really – it's not like he was blameless in this whole situation.

"So you're here because..." Dad folded his arms and looked at me expectantly. He knew I wasn't there to make nice.

"I need your help." Man, I hated saying those words.

Dad's eyebrows rose. "So...you're willing to talk to me when you need help, but not any other time?"

I didn't blink. "For the time being, yes."

We stared at each other for several seconds. Finally, Dad's shoulders sank slightly. "What do you need, Princess?"

The childhood nickname threw me off guard and made me hesitate a few seconds in my reply.

"I need my college money."

Dad had picked up a glass of water and taken a sip. Now, he choked on it and began coughing, his hand to his chest. "I'm sorry, what?" he asked when he could breathe again.

"I need my college money." I stood calmly, my hands wrapped around the strap of my purse, but inside I was shaking. I had never dared to stand up to my parents before, and had done so to both of them in the last week. It felt surreal, and completely...wrong. Except I knew I was right.

Dad set the glass down and moved past me, running a hand through his hair.

"How much is in my college account?" I pressed, knowing it was pretty substantial.

Turning to look at me, my father sized me up, then said, "About three hundred grand."

It was my turn to choke. "For – what – where did you think I would go to college, Dad? Geez!"

Dad gave a lopsided grin. "Harvard, Yale, somewhere like that. Neither law nor med school is cheap."

Figures. Dad had never been able to accept that I loved to write, that it was my passion. Every time I tried telling him that I wanted to pursue a career in writing, he cut me off and started shouting statistics about how much lawyers and doctors make. Like I cared.

"Okay, whatever. I need it."

Dad put his hands up in front of him. "Hold on there, Princess. You mind telling me what you need that much money for?"

"Yes."

My father stared at me. I sighed.

"For a friend."

"I'm not giving your education away to a friend," Dad said as an eyebrow inched up to his hairline.

"I can work to get through school. He needs this."

"Not that much, he doesn't."

I didn't see any way around it; I had to tell the truth.

"I have a friend who is about to be deported. If he has that money, he can get his student visa and attend the college he wants to here in the States."

Dad stared at me.

"He would be able to help his family, Dad." Exasperated, I threw my hands up in the air. What did he not *get*?

"So, this friend is here illegally?"

"Yes." My jaw jutted out defiantly, daring him to say anything else.

Sighing, Dad looked away, then back at me again. "I'm sorry, Princess, but I'm not going to have my daughter work through college and graduate with debt so some illegal alien can sweep through college on my money."

"Dad, you don't understand-"

Holding up a hand, Dad shook his head. "I understand enough. The answer is no."

My hands were shaking as my fingers dug into the strap of my bag. *Never good enough, never good enough.* That phrase kept pounding in my head. I wasn't able to help Veronica; I *would* help Wallace, no matter what I had to do to make that happen. I stared at my father, not really believing what I was about to do.

"You and Mom are going to get divorced, aren't you?"

Dad blinked, thrown off by the abrupt change in topic. "Yes, I'm afraid so."

The words were still like a punch to the gut, even though I had been expecting them. *Stay strong,* I mentally chided myself. *This is for Wallace.*

I took a deep breath and looked my father right in the eye. "It's going to be pretty ugly, isn't it? I mean, from what Hailee and I have seen so far, you and Mom are going to fight a lot."

Wincing, Dad turned his head away for a second before looking back at me. "Look, your mom just doesn't understand-"

I held my hand up to cut him off. "I'm not going there," I said, shaking my head. I waited until he looked me in the eye again. "My question to you is, how do you think Mom will react when she finds out that Marin," I spit out the name of Dad's secretary like it was a bad taste in my mouth, "wasn't your first indiscretion?"

Dad's face paled, and I felt my stomach twist. No matter how mad I was at my father, he was still my dad, and I was threatening to destroy him. I made myself continue.

"That, in fact, Marin is only the most recent of several? And who do you think the judge will side with when he finds that out?"

My dad's face went from white to beet red in three seconds flat. "Let me get this straight," he said, his voice dangerously low. "My daughter is *blackmailing* me to get hundreds of thousands of dollars to *give away* to a friend – one who isn't even in the country legally."

I pretended like I was thinking it over, then gave a short nod. "Yeah, that about sums it up."

Dad gave a short laugh. "And you said you don't want to be a lawyer."

"Not wanting to be a lawyer and the ability to be a good one aren't the same thing."

A look crossed my father's face, almost like he had never seen me before. I turned off my emotions and leaned forward. Speaking very slowly, I made sure he knew I wasn't kidding around.

"Write the check, Dad."

Veronica

41.

I was freaking out. Seriously *freaking out*.

Then Priss called and said she thought she had the solution – a way for Ace to stay in the United States. She asked if she could pick me up in an hour, and I told her to get here faster.

It was noon, but I wasn't hungry; food didn't even enter my mind. It was the warmest Saturday we had had all spring, but I couldn't enjoy the sun or the flowers sprouting through the dirt.

When had Ace become so important to me? And when had Priss and I become the type of friends to text each other on a Saturday and pick each other up to go to a friend's house? The context of the visit didn't matter; it was weird.

I didn't have the answer to any of my questions, but I still raced out of the house when I saw Priss' car coming up the street. I waited at the end of the driveway, not even giving her time to pull in before opening the door and sliding into the seat. For once I didn't need all the answers; I just needed to keep the people I suddenly cared about from leaving me.

Priss stared at me as I wrestled one-handed with the seatbelt. "What happened to your hand?"

"This?" I waved my stiff right arm, encased in a black fiberglass cast from forearm to fingertips. "Turns out Liam's face is harder than I thought."

I thought Priss would yell at me, but when I looked over, a slow grin spread across her face. "Nice," she said, nodding her head.

No matter how hard I tried, I couldn't get Priss to tell me what her plan was. She stubbornly remained mute until we pulled into Ace's driveway. Then she turned to me, her eyes bright.

"We can do this," Priss said. "We can save Wallace. Okay?"

Wanting to believe her, I nodded. Ace was surprised when his mom opened his bedroom door and told him we were there. She let us move past her into the room, but left the door open when she went back to the living room. Ace simply looked at us, and it scared me how tired he looked. Almost like he had given up.

Since looking at him made my stomach twist in knots, I looked around the room, noting how different Ace's and Mateo's tastes were. Mateo obviously liked comic books and graphic novels; Ace had breathtaking posters of skyscrapers and blueprints of famous buildings as they were being built.

"Wallace, I have a way for you to stay in the United States." Priss jumped right in, and I was thankful for that; I needed to hear the plan before I completely fell apart.

Ace continued to regard us without much expression, and I felt my stomach twist again. "Emma-"

Priss held up her hand. "Hear me out."

Ace sat back against his headboard, but didn't look as if he really wanted to.

"I'm giving you my college money." The words came out in a rush, and both Ace and I stared at her in surprise. *This* I was not expecting. "I looked it up – you can get a student visa and go to college here, but it will take about three to five months. The money will be enough to live off of *and* pay your way through college. You won't even have to work!"

Ace managed to recover from his shock before I did. "Emma, that is really nice of you, but I'm not taking your college money. What are *you* going to do then?"

Waving her hand in the air dismissively, Priss didn't look the least bit worried. "My dad has plenty of money; it's good for him to learn to share. Besides, I'm not an invalid. I know how to work."

While part of me agreed with Ace, I wanted to yell at him to take the money and shut up. If he took the money, that meant I wouldn't lose him; he wouldn't go back to Mexico. Ace, however, stunned us both with his next words.

"We're not fighting the deportation."

He looked away from me as he said it, and I was glad. Tears immediately sprang to my eyes while at the same time I wanted to punch him in the face with my good hand.

"What? Why not?" Emma gasped.

Ace rubbed his hands down his face and sighed. "I didn't know this until this morning, but Papá has been in touch with family from Isla Mujeres."

"Where is that?" I asked, surprising all of us by speaking for the first time since we got there.

Ace's eyes softened as he looked at me. I had to look away now, feeling my chest squeeze painfully as I looked into his eyes.

"It's an island near Cancún. They need schools and homes there, badly. Papá has been thinking for several months now about moving back to help build. It would be steady work for several years as they have already raised the money from sponsors and online funding. They really need the help."

But I really need you, I wanted to yell.

"What about you, Ace?" I said instead. "What about your dream of being an architect?"

Ace smiled sadly. "They asked me to help design the buildings with the knowledge I already have. They will pay for this, which will help my family, and give me experience so it will be easier to find a job once I do complete my schooling."

"But *how?*" Priss burst out. "Do they even have architectural schools in Mexico? Or whatever they're called," she added, suddenly looking unsure that she had called it the right thing.

Ace took a deep breath. "I have been researching what classes I can take online to help start earning my degree while I am on Isla."

"They have good Internet connections there?" Priss was pressing hard, her face screwed up in concentration. "What about a computer? Does your family have one? I don't remember seeing one."

She was talking fast, and I could tell her mind was working, but I didn't know what she was trying to figure out. I could tell by the look on Ace's face that he was also trying to figure out what Priss was thinking.

"They have public places, like the libraries here, where they offer computers to use, with Internet access."

"Is it free?" Priss looked like her mind was a million miles away.

Ace shook his head. "No, you pay a small fee to use them."

Priss paused. Then she looked at me. "We want you to stay," she finally said, turning back to Ace.

"I can't abandon my family," Ace said quietly, his eyes begging us to understand.

"Think of what that degree could mean to your family," I argued. "Once you have the degree and get a job, you can help them even more with the money you would make."

"What would they do during the four years I am gone getting that degree?" His voice wasn't scolding or angry, just matter-of-fact. "How do I help them while I am gone for those years?"

I didn't have an answer for that, and it pissed me off and made me feel helpless at the same time. I looked at Priss, silently begging her to talk some sense into him.

"There's no way we can talk you into taking the money and going to college here?" Priss' voice sounded resigned, and I didn't like that at all.

"I'm sorry."

The words were simple and quiet, but they were like a knife in my chest.

Wallace

42.

It killed me that I was hurting Veronica like this. There was pain and betrayal in her eyes, and I had never seen her so vulnerable. I willed her to look at me, but she had turned away, pretending to look at a poster of the Burj Khalifa in Dubai. I heard Emma sigh and turned to look at her.

"I'll be right back, don't move," she said, then walked quickly out of my room.

The silence felt deafening as Veronica continued to ignore me, staring blankly at a poster she didn't really see. I slowly got off the bed and walked closer. Her shoulders stiffened when she heard me, and I stopped.

"Veronica," I said softly.

"You said you weren't going anywhere."

The words were coated in ice, and my eyes closed, knowing with those words exactly how much I had hurt her.

"I can't leave my family, Veronica. Please try to understand." I was begging, but I didn't care. I had to make her understand.

She whirled to face me, her fists clenched. "But what about *you*? What about *your* dream of becoming an architect?"

"That may be *what* I want to be. Eventually. But *who* would I be if I left my family on their own for years while I selfishly pursued what I wanted?"

"You would be someone who cared enough about his family to get a good job and help support them," Veronica snapped angrily.

I stood still and looked at the spark of fury in her eyes. "I would rather be a son with honor who stood by his family, than someone who designs buildings for people I will never meet or know."

Veronica's jaw clenched, and I knew she wanted to argue.

"Would you like me as much if I stayed? Would you like who I was?"

"Yes! No – I don't know! That's not fair!"

Veronica burst into tears, covering her face with her hands, and I stepped forward to wrap my arms around her, being careful of her cast. I still couldn't believe she punched Liam. That text last night had almost been a bigger surprise than finding out we were going back to Mexico.

When Veronica's cries finally got quieter, I leaned back and gave her a half smile. "I hear long-distance relationships are all the rage now." She looked at me in disbelief, then pounded on my chest with her good fist. I kept my arms around her waist and she finally sagged back into me, her eyeliner and mascara making black circles around her eyes from the tears.

"Okay, here."

We both turned to see Emma walk back into the room carrying a slim purple case. If she was surprised to see Veronica in my arms, she didn't show it.

"What's that?" Veronica asked, leaning away from me and scrubbing at her cheeks with her hand.

"My laptop."

I stared at Emma, not quite understanding what she was getting at.

"It's yours, Wallace."

"Um, what?"

Emma set the case on the bed and unzipped it. Inside lay a Mac laptop, its top shiny and clean under my bedroom light. She reached into another zippered pocket and began pulling things out and dropping them on the bed.

"Here are all the manuals and software information, the charger, and an extra flash drive that I never use. Oh, and here's my password." Emma grabbed a manual and started scribbling. "You can change it to whatever you want." She looked down at everything spread out on the bed. "Sorry about the purple case, but you can get a new one if you want."

Once more, silence reigned.

I finally cleared my throat. "Emma, I can't take this."

Emma twisted her fingers together. "Yes, you can. If you won't take the money and stay, then you will take this and promise me you'll take the classes you need to start working toward your degree." She stared at me defiantly, but I could see tears in her eyes.

Suddenly Emma rushed at me, threw her arms around me, and squeezed tight. "You can't leave without saying good-bye. Promise."

"Promise." I hugged Emma to me, then she stepped back and wiped at her face with her hands, her sleeves coming away wet with tears. "I'll give you guys a minute." She walked out into the hall.

I turned back to Veronica.

"When do you leave?"

"Wednesday. Papá will inform the immigration people Monday that we are leaving by our own decision and will be gone by Wednesday."

"That's too soon."

I took Veronica's good hand in mine. "This isn't it for us, not if you don't want it to be." I bent until I could look into her eyes. "I'm willing to do the long-distance thing if you are." *Please be willing to,* I silently begged her. But I knew it wasn't fair to demand that of her.

After a pause, Veronica nodded, and I felt relief rush through me. "Promise?" she asked, so quietly I almost didn't hear. I pulled her toward me and put my arms around her again, resting my cheek against her hair.

"Promise," I whispered.

Emma

43.

I felt like I had a migraine.

After dropping Veronica off at her house, I drove straight home and went up to my room. Sitting cross-legged in the middle of my bed, I stared sightlessly at the blue wall across from me. This sucked. A lot.

I don't know how long I sat there, but after a while Hailee knocked on the door and stuck her head around the edge. "Can I come in?"

Nodding, I watched as she came over and sat facing me on the bed, pulling her legs up to cross them like mine. We stared at each other.

"What's going on?"

It was like a dam burst, and the whole story about the sociology project, Wallace and Veronica, and the deportation came flooding out. I hoped it would feel better to get it all out, but I only felt worse, even more tired, and my head pounded even harder by the time I was done.

Hailee sat in silence for a minute. "So he's really leaving?"

I nodded. "I failed, yet again," I said bitterly.

Her eyes narrowing, Hailee stared at me. "What does that mean?"

Shaking my head, I looked away. "I couldn't make him stay, just like I couldn't help Veronica graduate, just like I don't have a chance of making valedictorian or getting my writing published."

Hailee was quiet for so long, I finally looked back at her. "What?"

"Dad really did a number on you, didn't he?"

My forehead creased in confusion. "What are you talking about?"

Hailee shifted on the bed, leaning forward slightly. "Em, you are super smart and an awesome writer. The school paper is always asking for your stuff."

I shrugged. "But not the youth lit magazines I send stuff in to."

Hailee shook her head. "Yet. But they will. And who cares about being valedictorian anyway? Seriously, who needs that pressure?" She rolled her eyes and made a face, and I couldn't help but laugh.

"Don't you get it, Em? You're not perfect; no one is perfect. Who wants to be? That would be so *boring*." She made another face and I smiled. "Veronica isn't graduating because she didn't do the work she was supposed to. Wallace is leaving of his own choice. You can't control them, and they can't control you. It has nothing to do with failing."

I stared at my little sister in amazement. "When did you get so smart?"

Hailee squinted at me. "I should probably be offended by what that just implied, but I'll choose not to be."

Laughing, I grabbed a pillow and threw it at her. "You know what I mean!"

Smiling, Hailee hugged the pillow to her chest. "It actually sounds kind of cool, what Wallace and his family are doing."

Sighing, I nodded. "Yeah, it does. They are an amazing family. I just wish I could do more to help them."

Hailee shrugged and got off the bed, heading toward the door. "Maybe you can, but just haven't found the way that works yet." She tossed the pillow back to me.

Catching the pillow in mid-air, I suddenly froze, the pillow suspended above the bed. *Maybe you can, but just haven't found the way that works yet.*

"Hailee, you're a genius," I muttered, throwing the pillow on the floor. I reached for the notebook I always kept next to my bed. Gripping the pen so hard it hurt, I began writing, my mind racing faster than my hand could move.

Veronica
44.

I still couldn't believe Wallace was gone. He should have been standing right beside me, helping give the presentation that was based on his family. Instead, he was on the island of Isla Mujeres, designing schools and houses, probably even swinging the hammer himself.

Priss clicked the small remote in her hand, switching to the next slide in the PowerPoint presentation. "What people don't realize is that diabetes has reached epic proportions on the island of Isla, as well as in other areas of Mexico…"

I tuned her out, even though the next slide was mine. I had rehearsed what I was going to say until I was blue in the face, for the first time actually caring what grade I got on an assignment. It had stressed me out so much I went back to smoking. Until Priss found out and stole my cigarettes, breaking them in half and flushing them down the toilet.

Priss looked at me, and I realized it was my turn to talk. "Um, so education is really important, not only for jobs or careers, but for their health. However, they don't view education quite the same way we do…"

It took a minute, but I finally found a rhythm and talking felt easier. Priss kept smiling at me, probably to encourage me, but it made me even more nervous, so I ignored her. What shocked me was how much of the class was *listening*. They actually seemed interested in what we were talking about.

When we finally got to the end of the presentation, Priss set the remote down and clasped her hands in front of her. I knew what she was going to say; we had talked so much about what to say and how to say it that we both could recite it in our sleep.

"Everyone knows that our partner in this project, Wallace Perez and his family, were all deported back to Mexico several days ago."

Now we had *everyone's* attention. Even Ms. Hawthorne raised her head from grading papers and stared at us.

"So many families are being told they have to go back to their home country, no matter what the circumstances there may be, simply because they do not have the money or time needed to acquire a visa to enter the United States legally. It would seem like a simple thing to do, but so many families find themselves in situations they weren't expecting, making it harder to follow the rules. Instead of criticizing these families, Veronica and I are hoping you will help *us* help *them*."

I grabbed the remote and flipped to the very last slide of the PowerPoint, the one we added at the last minute.

"This is the web address for our blog," Priss said, glancing up at the screen as it flashed to life again. "It's called Ace in the Hole. We decided on this name because we believe that if we all help, it will create a widespread movement that will have more ripple effects than we can imagine, reaching families all over Mexico."

I saw a few people write down the name and web address in their notebooks, even Ms. Hawthorne. I took over, making sure my voice sounded strong.

"There are many individual essays on the blog, written by Pr – Emma – that give information on the greatest needs in the Mexican culture, and how we can best help. You can also find links to funding pages we set up that specifically target the need for medical help, food, shelter, and the application fees for obtaining visas."

Seriously, I had never used such big words or talked with such careful phrasing in my life. I hoped I didn't sound as stupid as I felt.

Priss stepped forward, her face earnest. "Please share this blog with everyone you know. Social media is a force all its own, and we can really make a difference if we are willing to try."

"Thank you," we chorused at the end.

I felt my whole body sag with exhaustion, and I was caught off guard by the desire to cry. I wanted Ace, I wanted to feel his arms around me, and I wondered what he was doing right then. We texted, called, and emailed every day, but it wasn't the same, and I couldn't believe how much I missed him.

Priss tossed her arm around my shoulders, ignoring the astonished looks of her friends, Sami, Tiffany, and Ben. As we wove through the desks toward the back of the classroom, Ian held up his hand as we passed and Priss slapped him a high five.

As we slid into our seats, Priss leaned over, her eyes bright with excitement. "Chin up, Veronica."

I looked at her in surprise. Then my eyes narrowed. She was up to something, I could tell.

Priss grinned. "You're going to love what I have planned next."

Emma

45.

I unzipped both carry-ons, making sure both laptop computers were snug in their cases. Then I reached into my purse and took out the two boarding passes for the plane to Mexico that I had already looked at fifty times.

"Would you stop? You're freaking me out more than I already am, Priss."

Glaring at Veronica, I shoved the tickets back in my purse. "I just want to make sure we have everything."

I sat back in my seat, tapping my fingers on my leg while Veronica licked her finger and turned another page in her magazine. Suddenly I sat up straight. "You did sign up for the online classes, right? So you could finish your diploma over the summer?"

Veronica turned another page in her magazine, refusing to look at me. "Yes. And you've asked me that four times already."

"Excuse me for caring," I huffed, flopping back in the hard airport chair and crossing my arms. "It's cool that your mom is taking classes too," I offered after a couple minutes of silence.

Veronica grunted, and I rolled my eyes.

"Hailee okay with you leaving?"

Oh, *now* she would talk. "Yeah." I paused, picking at a loose thread on my shorts. "I told her that if it gets bad again, I'll fly her out and she can stay with me."

"What about Ian?"

I smiled. "He's okay with it all. He's planning to come visit in July."

Veronica tossed the magazine on the chair next to her. "I can't believe our parents are okay with us doing this. Especially since it's the day after graduation."

"Well, I didn't say my parents were *excited* about it…" I pulled harder at the string, finally tearing it loose. I balled it up between my fingers. "But I'm eighteen, so what can they do?"

Veronica turned her head to the side and glanced at me. "They can cut off your trust fund."

I smirked. "Yeah, but I still have the college money – minus a couple plane tickets and computers," I said, grinning at her.

Veronica grinned back. "Yeah, but 'fess up. You already have all that money earmarked for certain projects on Isla."

I blushed. "Maybe," I said defensively. But I wasn't really upset. Veronica and I had already talked through what that money was going toward to help the people in Mexico, so I knew she was just kidding.

Neither one of us was ignorant of what was coming. A lot of hard work, homesickness, and tears. But we were ready to take on the world. Or, at least, Mexico.

"I still can't believe how much money we've raised through your blog," Veronica said, tilting her head back to rest on the back of the seat. "How many followers are there now?"

"One hundred thousand, two hundred and thirty-five."

Veronica laughed, still staring at the ceiling. "You crack me up, Priss."

I leaned my own head back on my seat. "You ever going to stop calling me that?"

"Probably not."

We both sat quietly, listening to the PA announcements, babies crying, and suitcase wheels rolling down the corridor.

"I'm proud of you, Priss."

"What?" That got my head up off the chair.

Veronica rolled her eyes, still looking at the ceiling. "Don't make a big deal out of it, geez."

"Sorry," I put my head back down. Then I glanced at her out of the corner of my eye. "But…what did you mean?"

Veronica shrugged. "Look at what you've done. Thousands of people are reading your blog and wanting to help other people. Not to mention the five newspaper articles you've written on the needs of families in Mexico – articles that have been *published*."

I felt a zing of excitement at her words. "I love knowing that what I'm writing is helping other people. I really hope it helps, anyway."

"It helps."

Silence settled over us. Ten minutes later, our flight was called to board. As we stood up and adjusted straps over our shoulders, Veronica and I looked at each other. Taking a deep breath, I took the one-way boarding pass from my bag and handed Veronica hers.

"You ready for this?" I asked as we eyed the gate that would take us far away from everything we had known our whole lives.

"Totally ready."

We walked toward the terminal gate and handed our boarding passes to the flight attendant.

Wallace
46.

The humid air swirled around me and made my shirt stick to my skin as I parked the truck and headed for the door leading into the airport. I didn't bother to lock the truck. It was a death trap, rusted and on the verge of falling apart. If someone wanted to steal it, they were welcome to it. At least the airport was air-conditioned.

I couldn't believe I would see them in just a few minutes. I scanned the signs, finally finding the gate where they would come in. Sitting down in a plastic chair in the baggage claim area where I would meet them, I immediately jumped to my feet again, unable to sit still.

It felt like it took forever, but finally I saw their plane number flash on a monitor above a baggage carousel; their plane had landed. I kept my eyes glued to the walkway, every new face that appeared making my stomach jump before my mind registered that it wasn't them.

Then they were there.

I felt a huge grin stretch across my face as I saw Veronica for the first time in three months. She smiled back, tossing her dark hair over her shoulder as she hiked up the strap to her carry-on bag. Emma appeared behind her, waving enthusiastically and almost dropping her purse.

I felt a shift in the universe just then, as if it was gearing up for what was to come. *Hold on, universe,* I thought as I started forward. *You have no idea what we're capable of.*

This was going to be *awesome.*

"I still don't know for sure who I am, but I'm starting to figure it out. So far I'm okay with it."
-Veronica

"I never thought I'd be here, but I love it."
-Emma
"Really? Cause it's freaking hot, and you sweat like a pig, Priss."
-V
"Seriously? Can't you ever say something nice?"
-E
"You love me anyway."
-V
"Maybe."
-E

"We are wiser and stronger because of the hardships we faced."
-Wallace
"You need to find your own sayings instead of copying your grandmother all the time."
-V
"You know you love it. And me."
-W
"XOXO"
-V

Author's Note

While a work of fiction, this book deals with issues we all face day to day. From struggling to feel "good enough," to the pressures of society that blur the lines between recognizing *who* we are is more important than *what* we are, or what job we hold.

A visit to Mexico in 2017 directly impacted my plan for *The Rejects of Room 5,* bringing to life for me the sense of community the people there hold dear. It also brought to life real struggles and hardships otherwise easy to ignore from an ocean away. My hope is that this novel will remind us all to withhold judgment; there is no way to know a person's true story until we have seen it with our own eyes.

There are many special people in my life who are a large part of my writing career, and deserve the utmost thanks.

Thank you to Rachel, for allowing me a glimpse into the truth of another culture. As always, a big thank you to Tom and his honest evaluation of my work. This book would not be where it is today if not for my editors: Matt, Karl, Marge, and Rae. I appreciate your work behind the scenes!

D. A. Reed lives in West Michigan with her family. Her inspirational young adult novels are based on challenges children and adults face every day, and her characters touch the hearts of readers even after the last page has been turned. Hopefully the message her novels contain will help and encourage those who read them.

Other works by D. A. Reed include YA novels *Daisies in the Rain* and *Dancing with Shadows,* as well as four works of the thriller genre: *Web of Deceit,* the forthcoming *When Darkness Killed Her* (full-length novels), *Toxic Love* and *Truth or Die* (novellas). All of her books are ready for purchase on Amazon and www.lulu.com. Find out more about D. A. Reed at www.facebook.com/Author/Deborah.